A
JOYFUL NOISE™
MEDALLION
BOOK

PRESENTED TO

Mom

FROM

Gale

DATE

3-1-96

My Bedtime Anytime

STORYBOOK

A
JOYFUL
NOISE™
MEDALLION
BOOK

My Bedtime Anytime

STORYBOOK

WRITTEN BY

V. GILBERT BEERS

ILLUSTRATED BY

TIM O'CONNOR

THOMAS NELSON PUBLISHERS
Nashville • Atlanta • London • Vancouver

Published in Nashville, Tennessee, by Thomas Nelson, Inc., Publishers, and distributed in Canada by Word Communications, Ltd., Richmond, British Columbia.

ISBN 0-7852-7725-0

Printed in the United States of America
2 3 4 5 6 7 – 00 99 98 97 96 95

C O N T E N T S

CONTENTS CONTINUED

A NOTE TO PARENTS AND TEACHERS

Welcome to a friendly little community that can exist only in your imagination, and in the imagination of your child. Here lives an unlikely little band of friends who come from everywhere, yet nowhere.

McWhiskers is a talking, larger-than-lifesize mouse—a wise, insightful, fun-filled little fellow who keeps his larger friends on track.

Tux is a penguin-away-from-penguinland.

KaWally is a koala from lands down under somewhere—how far down under, and under where, nobody knows.

PJ looks like a zebra, but unlike the ordinary zebras you know, he walks on two legs, not four, and like his friends, talks and thinks unzebralike thoughts.

Bru is a moody, grouchy-at-times-but-lovable-at-all-times bruin bear from somewhere north of nowhere. You can't help loving him, even though he sometimes tests the patience of his friends. Bru isn't bad. He is, well, almost human!

And then there is the world's only blue hippo—big, lovable, cuddly (if you could get your arms around him) Puddles. He is a hippo like no other hippo. Although you and I aren't blue hippos, we relate to so many of the things Puddles says and thinks—which says you and I are either more like blue hippos that we want to admit, or Puddles is more like people than he wants to admit. We will leave it to your imagination to decide which is true.

In this special imaginary land the creatures are conscious of their Creator, and occasionally burst into praise to Him. They are also conscious of those values that are woven into the fabric of the best of human character. If you encounter joy or wonder or imagination or delight, please do not be surprised. If you want to linger with these special friends and delight in their experiences, do not be surprised. If your child wants to walk back through the pages of this book again and again and make Bru, Puddles, McWhiskers, Tux, KaWally and PJ his or her own special friends, do not be surprised.

So walk with us into that fun-filled, yet highly educational land with its unlikely little community of friends who call themselves JOYFUL NOISE.[TM] One trip through this delightful land will never be enough.

—*V. Gilbert Beers*

A   J O Y F U L   N O I S E[TM]   M E D A L L I O N   B O O K

Joyful Noise™ *for Girls and Boys*

With horns to toot
  And songs to sing,
With things that clang
  And some that ring,
We prance and dance
  On tippy toes,

And make a happy sound
That grows.
We sing a song
For girls and boys,
So you may call us
Joyful Noise.™

Puddles and His Problem

A Story About Forgiveness

Puddles had a problem. It wasn't really a big problem. It certainly would not be a big problem for you. But Puddles thought it was a big problem. So if he thought it was a big problem, it really was a big problem to him.

"What shall I do?" Puddles asked himself. But of course Puddles couldn't answer his own question. If he could, he wouldn't have asked it in the first place, would he?

"Whatever shall I do?" Puddles asked again, not once, but many times.

Puddles decided that he would ask some friends what to do. Perhaps they would know.

Puddles ran off to find his friend Bru. A big bruin bear ought to know what to do about anything. If the biggest bear he had ever met (of course he hadn't met any other big bears) couldn't answer his question, who could?

Bru was sitting under a big tree, practicing on his horn. He was having so much fun that he didn't even see Puddles. So

Puddles stood politely, waiting for Bru to see him.

But Bru kept on practicing on his horn. At last Puddles grew tired of waiting. He reached down and pulled Bru's horn right out of his hands.

"What did you do that for?" Bru asked angrily. "You interrupted my important work!"

"Sorry, Bru," said Puddles. "But I have a problem. I thought you might have an answer."

"Of course I have an answer," said Bru. "I'm the smartest bruin bear around here." Puddles had to think about that. He really didn't think there *were* any other bruin bears around there. But why argue with a friend, especially if you want that friend to help you.

"Well, what is your problem?" Bru asked impatiently. "Or do you want me to answer your question before you ask it?"

Puddles didn't know how to answer that, so he told Bru his problem.

"Someone did something bad to a good friend," said Puddles. "So what should the good friend do to the person who did something bad?"

"Huh?" Bru asked. "Say that again."

Puddles said it again. He even said it four times before Bru knew what he said.

Bru jumped up. He grabbed his horn from Puddles. He gave a powerful blast on it. The powerful blast almost knocked Puddles from his feet. "I'd blast that guy!" said Bru. "I'd blast him so hard he would never do something bad to me again. Do you hear me? Blast him!"

Puddles didn't think that was the answer he wanted. So he politely thanked Bru and hurried off to find another friend.

Bru sat down and began practicing on his horn again. Before long Puddles found PJ, taking an afternoon nap. Puddles stood for a long time, waiting for PJ to wake up. But he didn't. Puddles supposed zebras don't wake up as easily as other animals. So Puddles decided to wake him.

"HEL-L-L-O-O-O!" Puddles shouted as loud as he could right into PJ's left ear.

PJ jumped up. Puddles thought he almost flew up. PJ looked round angrily, as if he was ready to fight.

"Where is he?" he shouted. "Where did he go?"

"Who?" asked Puddles.

"Whoever woke me," said PJ. "I'll beat him up."

Of course Puddles didn't want to get into a fight with PJ. He wanted PJ to help him.

"I'm sorry, PJ," said Puddles. "I'm really very sorry to wake you. But I need your help."

"Anything for you, old buddy," said PJ. "What can I do for you?"

"Help me know what to do about my problem," he said.

Then Puddles asked PJ the same question he had asked Bru.

"Someone did something bad to a good friend," said Puddles. "So what should the good friend do to the person who did something bad?"

"What's the problem?" asked PJ. "People are always doing bad things to me. I'd tell the good friend to forget it. It's just tough luck. You win a few and you lose a few, right? No problem. That's just the way life is."

But that didn't seem like the right answer to Puddles either. So he thanked PJ and went off to look for another friend. When he looked back, PJ was already taking his nap again.

Before long Puddles found his friend McWhiskers struggling to carry corn in a wheelbarrow.

"Afternoon, Puddles," said McWhiskers. "What can I do for you?" McWhiskers stopped working and shook hands with Puddles.

"You can help me with my problem," said Puddles.

"Glad to help you, old friend," said McWhiskers. "Tell me all about it."

So Puddles told McWhiskers what he had asked his other two friends.

"Someone did something bad to a good friend," said Puddles. "So what should the good friend do to the person who did something bad?"

"That's easy," said McWhiskers. "He should forgive his good friend."

"Forgive him?" asked

Puddles. "Is it that easy?"

"Of course," said McWhiskers. "But of course the other guy should ask him to do it."

"Whew!" said Puddles. "It's really that easy? Then I'm asking you to forgive me. I told some friends you were a little squirt. But I don't think that was very nice for me to do that. So will you forgive me?"

McWhiskers hated to be called a little squirt. If you can think of the nastiest, meanest thing that someone could call you, you know how you would feel if someone called you that name. That's how McWhiskers felt about being called a little squirt.

"Little squirt, huh?" said McWhiskers. "You know how I hate for people to call me that, don't you?"

"I do," said Puddles. "And I'm really very sorry. I'm even very, very sorry. But you also said you should forgive me if I ask you."

"Then I guess I had better forgive you," said McWhiskers. "And I do. But I'm sure you'll never call me that again, will you?"

"Never, little—," Puddles caught himself before he said little squirt again. "Never, old friend."

Then Puddles took off the whole afternoon to help his old friend McWhiskers move his corn.

23

STRIPES AND SPOTS

*A Story
About Worry*

"Why do I
have to wear
stripes?" PJ
asked himself.
"Look at Puddles
and Bru and Mc-
Whiskers and Tux
and KaWally.
Not one of
them has
stripes. They
make me look

like I'm a referee."

PJ looked in the mirror. But he quickly looked

away. He saw twice as many stripes now.

By this time PJ was beginning to have a pity party. He was feeling sorry for himself.

There is nothing like a good snooze to make a zebra feel better, PJ thought. *I'll crawl behind this big bush and sleep where nobody will see me and my ugly stripes.*

PJ was almost asleep when he heard voices on the other side of the bush. He listened carefully. Puddles and Bru were whispering.

"Did you get the paint?" Puddles asked.

"Yes," said Bru. "It's about as red as I

could find. We can paint some wonderful red spots with it. But we'll have to do it while he is sleeping. Won't he be surprised when he wakes up?"

PJ wasn't sleeping now. He was wide awake.

My friends! PJ thought. *My very own friends. They're going to paint red spots all over me while I'm sleeping.*

PJ looked at his black-and-white stripes. Then he thought about red spots. PJ thought how terrible the red spots would look. The black-and-white stripes looked better already.

What shall I do? PJ wondered. If he got up now, his friends would see him. Then they would know that he had heard what they said. PJ decided that he would lie quietly until his friends left.

PJ didn't have long to wait. In less than a minute Puddles and Bru walked off together, laughing. "Won't he be surprised?" Bru said with a big laugh.

"I can't wait to see him," said Puddles. Then both of them laughed again as if they had just heard a big joke.

PJ really felt sorry for himself now. Even worse, he didn't trust his friends. So he tried to stay away from them that day. But it's really

hard to stay away from big friends like Puddles and Bru.

That night PJ didn't want to go to sleep. He could hear Puddles and Bru chuckling and whispering. PJ tried to stay awake as long as he could, but finally he couldn't stay awake any longer.

Suddenly PJ heard a rooster crowing. He opened his eyes. The sun was up. It was morning. Then PJ quickly closed his eyes again.

"Oh, no!" PJ whispered to himself. "I fell asleep. I just know that Puddles and Bru painted red spots all over me."

PJ slowly opened his eyes again. Then he looked at himself. But was he ever surprised. There weren't lots of red spots on him. There wasn't even

one red spot. PJ saw nice black-and-white stripes all over him.

Then PJ heard McWhiskers talking. He was really excited.

"Oh, thank you, thank you, thank you," McWhiskers said. "I always wanted my little wagon painted with red spots. How did you know?"

"We only heard you say that a hundred times," said Bru. "Maybe even a hundred and one times."

"And your little wagon did need some paint," said Puddles. "It was getting quite ugly. So we bought the paint and painted it while you were sleeping."

PJ peeked around the corner. There was McWhiskers, pulling his little wagon covered with red spots.

"I guess I worried about something that never happened," PJ said when he told Bru and Puddles what had happened.

"Didn't you know? That's what worry is," said Bru. "But we do have enough red paint left to paint those red spots all over you if you wish."

"No thanks," said PJ, "I think black-and-white stripes are the most beautiful things in the world."

What do you think? Would you rather see PJ with his black-and-white stripes or red dots?

The next time you start to worry about something, you will remember PJ and his stripes, won't you?

The Big Red Ball

*A Story
About
Doing
Things
Together*

The big red ball that Bru bought was almost as big as McWhiskers. But when Bru felt mischievous and kicked the ball toward McWhiskers, the poor little fellow thought the ball was ten times as big as he.

"STOP DOING THAT!" Mc-Whiskers shouted each time.

But if you have ever known a mischievous bear like Bru, you know that wouldn't make him stop. If anything, it would make him do it all the more.

One morning McWhiskers

was pulling his little wagon on a narrow path going up a hill. Suddenly he saw the big red ball rolling down toward him.

McWhiskers didn't know the ball would not hurt him. So he jumped to the side of the path with his wagon.

McWhiskers and his wagon fell in a heap. Then he saw Bru, standing near the top of the hill, laughing as loud as a big bear can laugh.

"IT'S NOT FUNNY," McWhiskers shouted angrily.

That made Bru laugh even more.

"I WISH THAT OLD BALL WOULD BURST!" McWhiskers shouted at Bru. The big red ball was the kind that was filled with air, so it really could burst.

Bru frowned when he heard that. He didn't like to think of his beautiful red ball bursting.

"You don't really wish that," said Bru.

McWhiskers thought he really did wish that. He was angry and hurt that Bru kept rolling the big ball at him.

At noon, McWhiskers took a little picnic lunch out to the woods. He wanted to get away from Bru and his ball.

As you might guess, McWhiskers is a mouse, so he likes cheese. When he spread his little blanket on the ground, he opened his picnic basket and took out his cheese lunch.

A Swiss cheese sandwich, a Limburger cheese salad, and little chunks of mozzarella cheese for dessert were in the basket. What a picnic! You wouldn't like it, of course. But a happy mouse like McWhiskers thought it was something special.

"A quiet picnic away from Bru," McWhiskers whispered.

But McWhiskers had just picked up his Swiss cheese sandwich when he saw the big red ball rolling toward him.

"OH, NO!" he shouted. "Not here!"

McWhiskers jumped away from his picnic lunch as the big red ball rolled over it.

The lunch was such a mess!

Now he had a Swiss Limburger mozzarella messy mix.

"NOW LOOK WHAT YOU'VE DONE, YOU BIG, UGLY, OLD BEAR!" McWhiskers shouted.

But Bru only laughed. He didn't laugh as loud this time. But he did laugh.

"I HOPE THAT OLD BALL BURSTS," McWhiskers shouted. "I hope it bursts into a thousand pieces. I hope it bursts into a million pieces."

Bru frowned again when he heard that. "You don't really wish my beautiful ball would burst," he said.

McWhiskers almost wished he had not said that to his friend Bru. But Bru had been a terrible pest with his big red ball. McWhiskers really was

angry with Bru for rolling his ball at him. But he felt just a

little sad that he had said it.

That afternoon McWhiskers thought he would take a nap. It was the time of day when mice enjoy an afternoon nap, especially if they can find the right place.

McWhiskers thought he

would snooze near the rose bushes. He found a nice comfortable spot and stretched out. As soon as McWhiskers lay down and yawned, he saw the big red ball rolling toward him.

McWhiskers jumped out of the way, and the big red ball went rolling into the rose bushes. Bru had forgotten that rose bushes have thorns. McWhiskers had forgotten, too.

McWhiskers started to yell, "I hope that old ball bursts into . . ." But he couldn't finish.

The big red ball really did burst. There probably weren't a mil-

lion pieces, but there was one big mushy glob of red stuff.

Bru picked up the mushy red glob that had been his beautiful red ball. You have probably never seen a big bruin bear cry, but that's what Bru did. He sat down beside the rose bushes and cried as he looked at his mushy red glob.

McWhiskers felt sad now. He wished he had not said that about the red ball. He wished now that Bru had his wonderful big red ball, even if he was a pest about

rolling it at him.

Then McWhiskers had an idea. He ran home as fast as a mouse can run. Before long, he was back with Bru.

"Look what I have for you," he said.

Bru looked. It wasn't a big red ball. Little mice don't have those things. But it was a *nice* red ball.

"I have an idea," said Mc-Whiskers. "Instead of rolling balls at me, let's you and me play ball together." Bru thought that was a great idea.

You probably have never seen a bear and a mouse play-ing ball together. But if you could come to our place, that's what you would see. How soon can you be there?

The Bear Who Squeaked

A Story About Being Thankful for Who We Are

The other day Bru and Mc-Whiskers had an argument. It wasn't a knock-down-and-drag-out argument. It was an I-know-more-than-you argument. It all started when Bru said it must be easy to be a mouse.

"Nothing to do all day but snooze and eat cheese," Bru laughed. "What a soft life!"

"Not as soft as being a bear," McWhiskers snapped back. "Nothing to do but snooze and eat honey. What a soft life!"

Actually, neither Bru the bear nor McWhiskers the mouse knew what he was talking about. That's usually why arguments start, isn't it?

McWhiskers yawned when he said *snooze*. Even saying the word made him sleepy.

36

Bru yawned, too. Saying the word *snooze* made him sleepy, just like McWhiskers.

"Soft life...zzzzz," McWhiskers said with a big yawn.

"Soft life...zzzzz," Bru tried to answer.

But McWhiskers and Bru were both snoozing before they could finish the sentence.

As soon as he fell asleep, McWhiskers dreamed a strange dream. He wasn't a mouse at all. He was a bear, just like Bru. But he was a bear the size of a mouse. And he was very hungry.

"Honey! That's what I need," said McWhiskers in his dream. He started through the woods, looking for a honeycomb.

Before long McWhiskers the bear saw a large honeycomb in a big hole in the side of a big tree. "This will be easy," he said. So he started to scoot up the tree. But when he reached the honey, he saw that something else was there.

"Bees!" said McWhiskers the bear. "Millions of them! And they're coming after me."

McWhiskers the bear tried to

scoot down the big tree. But he was scooting so fast that he fell the last dozen or more feet with a big bump.

"OW!" he shouted.

Now the bees had caught up with him. McWhiskers the bear ran as fast as his legs could go. "Bzzzzz," went the bees. "Ow-w-w," went McWhiskers the bear.

You have never seen anyone run as fast as he ran. When McWhiskers saw a pond, he jumped into it and stayed under the water as long as he could. As soon as he poked his nose above the water, a bee stung him on the nose. Then the bees went away.

"OW-W-W!" shouted Mc-Whiskers the bear.

While McWhiskers was dreaming this strange dream, Bru was dreaming a strange dream, too. Bru the bear dreamed that he was a mouse. But in his dream he was a mouse as big as a bear. And he was very hungry.

"Cheese!" said Bru the mouse. "That's what I need! Lots of cheese."

Bru the mouse started out to look for some cheese. But before he could find cheese he met a cat. Bru the mouse was *much* bigger than the cat. But this didn't stop the cat. He called for all his friends. Suddenly there were dozens of cats. Now they were all chasing Bru the mouse.

Bru ran as fast as he could go. The cats ran as fast as they could go, too. The cats almost caught Bru when he saw a pond. He jumped into the pond and stayed under the water as long as he could. As soon as he poked his nose above the water, a cat scratched it. Then the cats ran away.

"OW-W-W!" shouted Bru the mouse.

Suddenly Bru the mouse saw McWhiskers the bear. He began to laugh.

"Look at you," he said. "A bear no bigger than a mouse. I've never seen anything so silly."

"But look at you," said Mc-

Whiskers the bear. "A mouse as big as a bear. I've never seen anything so silly."

Just then both McWhiskers and Bru woke up.

"You won't believe the dream I had," said Bru.

"And you won't believe the dream I had," said McWhiskers.

"But first I must find some honey," said Bru. "I'm hungry."

"And I must find some cheese," said McWhiskers. "I'm hungry, too."

Nobody knows if Bru or McWhiskers ever told each other their dreams. But McWhiskers was very thankful that he was a mouse. And Bru was very thankful that he was a bear.

And you are probably very thankful that you are you. If you aren't, you probably should be.

The Best Butterfly Catcher in the World

A Story About Pride

"**W**hatcha doing, little fellow?" Bru asked.

"Catching butterflies," said Tux.

"But where are they? I don't see any butterflies that you have caught," said Bru.

"OK, OK, I'm *trying* to catch butterflies," said Tux.

Bru looked around the meadow. There were lots of butterflies flying around. But Tux had not caught one.

"Good thing I came along," said Bru. "You need *me* to help you. I'm the best butterfly

catcher in the world. Maybe even better than that."

Without even asking, Bru grabbed the net from Tux and began to run around the meadow, chasing a butterfly.

"Keep your eyes on the butterfly," said Bru. "Don't look anywhere else. Keep your eyes on the butterfly—"

Bru stumbled over a big clump of dirt sticking up. He

fell headfirst. When Tux came to help him up, he almost laughed. The butterfly net had plopped over Bru's head. It looked like the net had caught Bru.

"We all make mistakes," Bru muttered. "Now watch me. I'm the best butterfly catcher in the world. Maybe even better than that."

Bru began running around the meadow as fast as he could go. "Keep your eyes on the butterfly," said Bru as he began chasing a butterfly. "Don't look anywhere else. Keep your eyes on the—"

Before he could say *butterfly*, Bru crashed into a tree. This time when Tux came to help him up, he saw the net caught on a tree limb above Bru.

"Crazy butterfly," Bru grumbled. "How did I know he would fly between the limbs of the tree."

Bru was a little woozy getting up. He didn't like it that a little fellow like Tux helped him up, but it did make it easier.

"All right," said Bru. "No scrawny little butterfly is going to do that to me. Here we go. Just remember, I'm the best butterfly catcher in the world. Maybe even better than that."

With that, Bru started off at top speed, chasing a butterfly. "Keep your eyes on the butterfly," said Bru as he ran as fast as he could go. "Don't look anywhere else. Keep your eyes on—"

This time Bru couldn't even say *the butterfly*. With a mighty crash he sprawled onto a big wood fence and went sailing over it, still holding his net. This time when Tux came to help him up, he did laugh. There was a big cow, bending over and licking Bru on the nose.

"Looks as if you found a new friend," said Tux.

"Oh, be quiet," Bru grumbled. "Here, go catch your own butterflies. I'm still the best butterfly catcher in the world, but I'm just a little tired today."

At that very moment a beautiful butterfly fluttered above Bru and Tux. With one gentle dive it came down and sat on Bru's nose, which was still wet from the cow.

"Oh, get out of here," Bru yelled at the butterfly.

"You caught one! You caught one!" said Tux. Bru stared cross-eyed at the butter-

fly, still sitting on his wet nose. "Why, so I did," he said.

Then Bru began to laugh at the way he caught the butterfly.

Of course this made Tux laugh, too.

But Tux never, never, never again heard Bru say that he was the best butterfly catcher in the world. Bru knew that his pride had caused him to fall three times. That was enough. Don't you think so?

47

Who Will Help the Kitty?

A Story About Helpfulness

"**L**ook! That poor kitty is on top of that old pole," said Tux. "We must help her."

PJ looked up at the kitty. She was certainly on top of the pole. And she wanted down. The kitty was wailing as loudly as she could.

"Something scared her," said KaWally. "Kitties run up a pole or a tree when they're scared. Then they don't know how to get down."

"Get Puddles," said Tux. "Maybe he can reach the kitty."

KaWally ran to get Puddles. But when Puddles reached as high as he could, he could not reach even halfway up the pole.

"Bru!" said Puddles. "Get Bru! Bears climb trees. He can climb up and get the kitty."

This time Tux ran off to find Bru. But when Bru looked up the pole he laughed. "You've got to be kidding," he said. "Bears climb trees. But they don't climb things like that old pole. No way!"

"Find McWhiskers," said KaWally. "He can climb things, too."

But as McWhiskers looked up the pole he shook his head. "I might be able to climb the pole," he said. "But what do I do then? I can't carry that cat down. She's as big as I am."

McWhiskers's friends knew that he was right. Of course he couldn't carry the kitty down all by himself.

"So what can we do? How can we help her?" asked PJ.

"I say leave the thing up there," said Bru. "Let her find her own way down."

"But she can't! She doesn't know how," said Tux. "And we can't just leave her there."

"Well, I have a ladder at my place," said Puddles. "That ought to do it." That seemed to

be a great idea, and so Puddles went home for his ladder.

But when Puddles propped his ladder against the pole, everyone saw that the ladder was little more than half as tall as it should be.

"I know," said KaWally. "Send up a balloon and let the kitty ride down on it." Everyone laughed. But no one thought that was a good idea.

Before long everyone had a suggestion. But the other friends did not like any of them.

Tux thought they should call the fire department. But where they lived there *was* no fire department. So who would they call?

PJ thought they should all

50

yell at the kitty and scare her so much that she would climb down. But being scared had only made her climb up before. Why would it make her climb down now?

Puddles thought they should put a bowl of milk near the pole. But the other friends said if she couldn't climb down to save herself, why would she climb down just to get some milk?

KaWally said they could hold a big sheet and tell the kitty to jump in it. But the other friends thought the kitty wasn't that brave.

"I still say leave the thing up there," said Bru. But his other friends looked at him angrily, and so he decided that wasn't a good idea either.

McWhiskers didn't say anything. He sat on the grass thinking about the problem.

"OK, what's your brilliant plan?" asked Puddles. "We can almost hear you thinking."

"I do have a plan," said McWhiskers. "It will work, too. Bru will stand on Puddles's shoulders. PJ will stand on Bru's shoulders. KaWally will stand on PJ's shoulders. Tux is next, on KaWally's shoulders. I'll be on the top, helping the kitty get off the pole. None of us can rescue the kitty by ourselves. But if we each help the others, we can all do it together."

You should have seen these friends as they did what McWhiskers said. It was a mess. Bru wasn't too careful with his foot, and he squished it over Puddles's eyes. PJ had to hang on to Bru with all four legs. And the others were hanging

on for dear life at the top. But they did it. Before long Mc-Whiskers was on top. He was as high as the kitty on the top of the pole.

"IT WORKS!" he shouted. "Hang on! We're going to do it."

The kitty was so surprised to see a big mouse looking at her that she took a swipe at McWhiskers with her claws. "Do that once more, you silly old cat, and you'll stay up here all winter," McWhiskers yelled at the kitty.

The kitty calmed down when she heard that and let McWhiskers help her off the pole. Before long everyone, even the kitty, was safely back on the ground.

Then the kitty began to purr. That was her way of saying, "Thank you."

"See, Puddles," said McWhiskers. "Next time you're caught on top of a big pole, the kitty will help you get down."

Don't you think that would be funny to see Puddles sitting on top of a tall pole? His friends did. I think they may still be laughing.

Surprise!

A Story About Kindness

"SURPRISE!" the little note read. "MEET ME AT THE OLD WELL DOWN THE ROAD."

McWhiskers twitched his whiskers. "Whatever can it mean?" he asked. "Who would have a surprise for me? Why? When? How?"

McWhiskers almost threw the little note into his waste basket. But like all mice, he was too curious.

"Why not find out?" he said to himself. "What harm could there be? If I don't go, I'll always wonder what it was all about. I'll probably not even sleep tonight. I might never sleep again."

That convinced McWhiskers that he should go where the note said. So off he went, down the road to the old well.

But no one was there at the well. No one!

"I've been tricked," said McWhiskers. "I'm going home."

But just as he turned to leave, he heard a voice. "Don't go home," said the voice. It almost sounded as if it came from the bottom of the well. "Go to the big tree down at the corner. You'll be sorry if you don't."

McWhiskers looked around. He could not see one person. Who spoke to him. Why? Where? Now he really was curious.

"I...I can't go home now," he whispered to himself. "I must go down to the big tree to see what this is all about."

So off he went, down the road to the big tree. But when he came to the big tree, no one was there. No one.

"I know I've been tricked this time," McWhis- kers said to himself. "Someone is playing a trick on me. I'm going home."

McWhiskers turned around and started home. But suddenly he heard a voice.

"Don't go home," the voice said. It almost sounded as if it came from the top of the big tree. "Go to the old train at the depot," the voice said. "If you don't, you will worry all night about the surprise and what you missed."

McWhiskers knew the voice was right. He couldn't go home now. He was too curious. So off he went to the train depot. There was the little steam loco-

motive sitting there as it has been for several years. It was the cutest old-fashioned miniature locomotive you've ever seen. It reminded people of the way trains looked many years ago. But there was no one waiting for McWhiskers.

"Someone is playing a trick on me," McWhiskers whispered to himself. "I know it. But who? Why? Now I really must go home." He turned and started back toward home.

But suddenly a voice called out. "You do want to sleep tonight, don't you?" the voice said. "Don't go home now. You'll worry about this surprise all night. Go to the picnic table at the park."

"He's right," said McWhiskers. "I know I won't sleep all night if I go home now. I simply *must* find out about this surprise."

So off he went to the picnic table in the park. But when he arrived, no one was at the picnic table. In fact, he didn't see anybody in the park.

"I really have been tricked," McWhiskers said. "Someone is trying to make me look silly. I must go home."

McWhiskers started home. But now he heard several voices. They seemed to come from the big trees in the park.

"Don't go home now!" the voices said. "Turn around."

McWhiskers turned around. He expected to see only the big trees. Instead he saw each of his friends, peeking from behind a big tree. Then they all came out. Some were carrying picnic baskets.

"Happy birthday to you! Happy birthday to you!" they all began to sing together.

"Why so it is," said McWhiskers. "I had forgotten that it's my birthday."

"SURPRISE! SURPRISE!" all his friends shouted.

Then McWhiskers's friends spread out a wonderful picnic lunch from their baskets. It almost filled the big table in the park.

"It certainly was tough hiding from you at each place," said Tux. "I had to talk into an old coffee can so you wouldn't know my voice."

"So it was you!" McWhiskers laughed.

Before long McWhiskers and friends sat down to the best birthday surprise lunch you have ever seen. Well, it's the best if you like lots of cheese. Cheese, of course, is the finest treat for a birthday mouse like McWhiskers. The birthday cake was even cheesecake.

Would you rather have lots of cheese than a birthday cake?

The Biggest Red Balloon

A Story About Pride

"Where did you get that scrawny little balloon?" Bru asked McWhiskers. Bru was sitting on a big stump by the side of the road, watching for his friends.

"It's not scrawny," said McWhiskers. "It's a cute little red balloon. I like it."

Bru bellowed with a big bear laugh. "It's scrawny," he teased. "Big tough bears like me would never be seen with such a scrawny, little, puny, shrimpy balloon."

McWhiskers didn't want to argue, and so he walked cheerily on the path, whistling as he went. He was gone for only a moment when PJ came along with a bigger red balloon. It wasn't really very big—certainly

not a PJ-size balloon—but you could tell he was happy.

"Where did you get that tiny little balloon?" Bru asked PJ.

"It's not that tiny," said PJ. "It's a nice middle-size balloon. Besides, I like it."

Bru bellowed again with a big bear laugh. "It's tiny," he teased. "Big tough bears like me would never be seen with such a tiny, little, shrimpy, scrawny balloon."

PJ didn't want to argue, and so he walked cheerily on the path, whistling as he went. He was gone for only a moment when KaWally came along with a bigger red balloon than the one PJ carried. And of course it was much bigger than the one McWhiskers carried.

"Where did you get that shrimpy little balloon?" Bru asked KaWally.

"It's not a shrimpy little balloon," KaWally said. "It's a nice KaWally-size balloon. I like it."

Bru bellowed again with a big bear laugh. "It's a shrimpy little balloon," he teased. "Big tough bears like me would never be seen with such a shrimpy, little, puny, scrawny balloon."

KaWally didn't want to ar-

gue, and so he walked cheerily on the path, whistling as he went. He was gone for only a moment when Tux came along with a much bigger red balloon. It was bigger than a Tux-size balloon.

"Where did you get that little balloon?" Bru asked Tux.

Tux looked at his red balloon. "You need to get your eyes fixed," he said. "This looks like a BIG red balloon to me."

Bru bellowed again with a big bear laugh. "It's a little balloon," he teased. "Big tough bears like me would never be seen with such a tiny, little, shrimpy, scrawny balloon."

Tux shook his head. He didn't want to argue with Bru, and so he walked cheerily on the path, whistling as he went. But Tux had just gone over a little hill when he saw McWhis-

kers with his tiny red balloon, PJ with his bigger red balloon, and KaWally with his still bigger red balloon.

"You're just in time," they all said. "We're going to have a red-balloon parade. Want to join us?"

Tux thought that was a great idea. But while he and his friends were laughing and getting in line for their red-balloon parade, they heard Bru laughing and coming toward them. When they looked, they saw Bru with the biggest red balloon they had ever seen. It was GIGANTIC. Under the GIGANTIC red balloon was Bru, hanging on for dear life as the balloon tried to take him up into the air. And Puddles was hanging on to Bru.

Actually, the red-balloon friends could see that it was Puddles who was keeping the GIGANTIC red balloon from taking Bru into the sky.

Bru was laughing a big bear laugh as he came toward his friends. "I told you that you all had tiny, scrawny, little, shrimpy balloons," he said. "This is a big bear balloon. None of that scrawny, little, shrimpy kid stuff for a real tough bear."

"Pride goes before a fall," McWhiskers whispered. But he said it softly so Bru wouldn't hear. He didn't want to hurt Bru's feelings.

A sudden gust of wind blew some dust in the air. This made Puddles sneeze. And when he sneezed, he let go of Bru.

Just as suddenly, the GIGAN-TIC red balloon began to carry Bru up into the air. Before Bru knew what was happening, he was as high as the treetops.

"HELP!" Bru shouted. "Someone get me down from here."

But the GIGANTIC red balloon kept on climbing.

"HELP!" Bru shouted, even louder this time.

All Bru's friends could do was watch with surprise. What else could they do? But they could see that Bru was frightened now.

Suddenly Bru's GIGANTIC red balloon burst. It was really something to see! Bru came tumbling down and fell into a

big pine tree. Then he tumbled into a thorny bush and sprawled onto the ground.

"BRU! BRU! ARE YOU HURT?" McWhiskers shouted as he ran to help him. All the other friends ran to help, too.

Bru had a little ragged piece of his red balloon draped over his head. He was scratched and bruised.

"I heard that!" Bru said to McWhiskers.

"Heard what?" McWhiskers asked.

"What you whispered be-

fore," said Bru. "Pride goes before a fall."

"Sorry about that," said McWhiskers.

"But you're right," said Bru. "I was too proud of my big red balloon. I even made

fun of you guys and your balloons. But you still have yours and I don't. And you're not all scratched."

"I have another red balloon at home," said McWhiskers. "It's not GIGANTIC. It's not

even big or middle size. It may not even be tiny. But you can have it."

So McWhiskers ran home to get his other red balloon. It really was a tiny, little, scrawny, shrimpy balloon. But you should have seen how happy Bru was, carrying it in a red-balloon parade with his friends.

A Bag of Clothes

A Story About Being Good

"What's this?" Puddles asked. He picked up a big bag by the side of the road.

Puddles and PJ peeked into the big bag. They were curious, just the way you probably would be if you found a big bag by the side of the road.

"Nothing but old clothes," said PJ.

Puddles laughed. "Old clothes," he said. "Let's surprise our friends with some of this stuff."

PJ thought that was a great idea. So he helped Puddles carry the big bag back home.

"Shhh," said Puddles. "We don't want them to know what we have yet. We'll have a pretend party."

So Puddles asked Bru, Tux, KaWally, and McWhiskers to sit on a big log. "We'll have a pretend party," he said. "PJ and I will pretend we are someone, and you must tell us who we are."

PJ found some hats in the bag. He put a big white cook's

hat on himself and a police officer's hat on Puddles. Then he and Puddles paraded out before their friends.

"What are we?" asked PJ.

"Goofy," said Bru. Then he laughed at his own joke.

"Come on," said Puddles. "We're having fun pretending. Pretend with us."

"PJ is a cook," said Mc-Whiskers. "Anyone can see that. But you need some pots and pans, PJ."

"And Puddles is a police officer," said Tux. "But you need a whistle, Puddles."

PJ and Puddles looked in the big bag. There were no pots and pans or whistles. But there were more old clothes. So Puddles put on an apron

and PJ carried some dish towels on his arm.

"What time is it?" asked Puddles.

"Time to stop this silly pretending," said Bru.

"Stop being a grump," said KaWally. "We're pretend- ing. So

loosen up and have some fun."

"I think it's time to wash the dinner dishes," said Tux.

"Very good," said PJ. "See how much fun pretending is."

"Let me try one," said KaWally. So he stood in front of them and stared up at the sky.

KaWally's friends stared at him. "What is he trying to do?" Tux whispered.

"He's doing nothing," said McWhiskers. "So he must be pretending that he's Bru."

"Ver-r-ry funny," said Bru. "Come on, KaWally. Tell us what you're pretending. We'll never guess it."

"Can't you see?" asked KaWally. "I'm pretending to be good."

All of KaWally's friends stared at him. "How can you pretend to be good?" they asked, "Either you're being good, or you're not being good."

"That's not true," said Bru. "Lots of people pretend that they're good when they're not."

"I think Bru's right," said Tux. "Most of us pretend to be good most of the time. But we're not as good as we pretend to be."

"Wouldn't it be awful if someone could see what we're really like and not what we pretend we're like?" asked PJ.

"Not if that someone could help us *be* good and *do* good instead of just *pretending* to be good and do good," said Mc-Whiskers.

"Do you suppose someone could really do that?" Puddles asked McWhiskers.

Do you know Someone who can do that? What would you like to ask Him right now?

The Magic Lamp
A Story About Greed

"What's that?" KaWally asked McWhiskers.

McWhiskers smiled as he pointed to an old brass vase in his wagon. "It's something special," he said. "I bought it at the flea market. The man said it might even be Aladdin's Lamp."

"Wow! Aladdin's Lamp!" said KaWally. "Do you know what he did? He rubbed the lamp and a genie came out.

The genie did anything Aladdin wanted. Let's rub the lamp and see what happens."

"Sorry, KaWally," said McWhiskers. "I'm saving it for some special time when I may need a genie to help me. Anyway, it may not be Aladdin's Lamp. The man just said it *might* be."

McWhiskers left KaWally with his mouth open as he pulled his little wagon with the

old brass vase behind him.

"Wait! I'll give you a pound of cheese for it," said KaWally.

McWhiskers laughed. "No, thanks," he said. And off he went.

But McWhiskers had not gone far when Tux came running after him. "Wait," he said.

"I want to see Aladdin's Lamp."

"It may not be Aladdin's Lamp," said McWhiskers. "The man said it *might* be."

"Wow, look at that!" said Tux when he saw the old brass vase in McWhiskers's little wagon. "Anyone can see it's Aladdin's Lamp. May we rub it?"

"Sorry, Tux," said McWhiskers. "I'm saving it for a special time."

"KaWally offered you a pound of cheese for it," said Tux. "I'll give you *two* pounds of cheese."

"No, thanks," said McWhiskers as he pulled his brass vase away.

But McWhiskers had not gone far when PJ came running after him. "Our friends said you have Aladdin's Lamp," he puffed. "May I see it?"

PJ's eyes grew big as he looked at the old brass vase. "It IS Aladdin's Lamp," he shouted. "I know it is."

"I don't know. The man only said it *might* be," said McWhiskers.

"Anyone can see that it is," said PJ. "Let's rub it and make ourselves rich. We'll share, of course."

"Sorry, but I'm saving it for a special time," said McWhiskers.

"Look, KaWally offered you a pound of cheese for it. Tux offered you two pounds of cheese for it. I'll give you *five* pounds of cheese for it," said PJ.

"No, thanks," said McWhiskers as he pulled his little wagon away with the brass vase in it.

But McWhiskers had not gone far when Puddles came running after him. "THE LAMP! THE LAMP!" he shouted. "I want to see Aladdin's Lamp."

"I have an old brass vase," said McWhiskers. "The man said it *might* be Aladdin's Lamp. I don't know if it is."

But when Puddles looked at the old brass vase, his eyes grew big. "Give it to me," he said. "I want to rub it and see the genie

come out. Think of all the money he could give us."

"Sorry, but I'm saving it for a special time," said McWhiskers.

"OK, let's get down to brass tacks," said Puddles. "I know KaWally offered you a pound of cheese for it. Tux offered you two pounds of cheese. PJ even offered you five pounds of cheese for it. Well, I'll give you *ten* pounds of cheese."

"And I'll give you *fifty* pounds of cheese for it," a voice said.

Puddles and McWhiskers looked up. They hadn't seen Bru come along. Bru had been watching. He had already seen the old brass vase.

"I said I'll give you *fifty*

pounds of cheese for that old cheap brass vase," said Bru.

"If it's an old cheap vase, why are you offering fifty pounds of cheese for it?" asked McWhiskers.

"Because he knows it's Aladdin's Lamp, that's why," said Puddles.

By this time, greedy Bru was slobbering. He was obviously so greedy to get the vase that his eyes were big and bright. And by this time, all of Bru's

and McWhiskers's friends had gathered around to watch what was happening.

"OK, OK, so it may not be Aladdin's Lamp," said Bru. "Let's stop messing around.
I'll give you *a hundred*

pounds of cheese for it."

"But it really is just an old cheap brass vase," said McWhiskers. "I want all of you to listen. It's just an old cheap brass vase."

"I said I'll give you *a hundred pounds of cheese* for Aladdin's...I mean, that old cheap vase," said Bru. Bru started to reach for the vase.

"Don't you dare touch that vase," said McWhiskers. "OK, I'll sell that old cheap vase to you for a hundred pounds of cheese, delivered to my house. But I want the cheese inside my door before you touch this vase."

Bru headed home with all his friends trailing behind him. But he was so eager to get the vase that he ran all the way. It was hard for his friends to keep up with him. Before long, he had a hundred pounds of cheese stacked up on his big wheelbarrow and was pushing it to McWhiskers's house.

When the hundred pounds of cheese were safely tucked behind McWhiskers's door, McWhiskers handed the vase to Bru. But the greedy old bear grabbed it from McWhiskers and ran behind a bush with it. All the friends ran after Bru to watch.

Bru sat down on the grass and rubbed his hands together. He was so happy. "I'll be rich! I'll have castles filled with honey," he gloated. "And to think that silly mouse sold it to me for a hundred pounds of cheese."

You should have seen Bru.

77

You would have been ashamed of him. He was so greedy that his eyes were now as big as saucers. And he was slobbering like a hungry bear.

Bru began to rub the vase. "OK, genie, come out and do your thing," he said. But nothing happened.

"Wrong words," he muttered. "I'll try again. ABRACADABRA, PLEASE AND THANK YOU!" But still nothing happened.

Bru kept rubbing the vase and saying different words.

But nothing ever happened.

"At least he's making the vase bright and pretty," said Puddles.

"If he doesn't rub a hole

through it first," said PJ.

"I told him it was just a cheap old vase, didn't I?" McWhiskers said to his friends. They all nodded. They knew now that Bru had been even more greedy than they had been. They were sure now that it was just a cheap old vase.

"You wait and see," said Bru. "I'll find the right words, and the genie will pop out."

"It's just a cheap old vase," McWhiskers whispered.

By evening all of Bru's friends went home. But during the night, someone would come out from time to time to see what was happening. All they ever saw was a lonely old bear rubbing a cheap old vase in the moonlight.

Some folks say he's still sitting there rubbing the cheap old vase that he bought for a hundred pounds of cheese. But others say that he sold it at a flea market for a hundred pounds of honey. No one knows for sure which story is right.

Do you?

Bru's Bad Day

A Story About Controlling Your Anger

Everyone has a bad day. Sometimes a bad day starts out that way. Sometimes it sneaks up on you between breakfast and lunch, or about the time you get to school.

So it was not a big surprise when Bru had a bad day. It's just that this bad day was really a bad day.

It all started early in the morning when Bru was cleaning his breakfast dishes. He was thinking about something else and dropped three of his best dishes on the floor. Of course, they broke into a dozen pieces. Bru said a hundred pieces, but bad days cause you to make things look worse.

Instead of sweeping up the broken pieces and throwing them away, Bru threw a tantrum. He screamed and yelled and pounded his fist on the table. He pounded the table so hard that he cracked one of the boards on the top.

Later, Bru was nailing a board on the side of his house. But the hammer slipped and hit his hand instead. Bru was so angry that he screamed and yelled and threw his hammer. But when people are really angry, they're not too careful where they throw things. So Bru accidentally threw his hammer through a window pane. The glass shattered into a hundred pieces. Bru said a thousand pieces, but you understand by now why he said that.

About the time Bru threw his hammer through the window, his friend KaWally came along. At first KaWally didn't know what to say. It really is hard to know what to say when a friend throws a hammer through his own window, isn't it?

"Bad day, Bru?" KaWally asked softly.

"SHUT UP, YOU OVER-GROWN STUFFED BEAR!" Bru screamed at his friend. "I don't need you around to give me advice. Beat it!"

"Just trying to be helpful," said KaWally. "You don't have to chew my head off. You really should learn to control your anger, Bru. It might get you into trouble, you know."

"GET OUT OF HERE!" Bru shouted.

KaWally could see that Bru really was having a bad day, and so he left quietly and went home. But he had just left when PJ came along.

"Someone break your window, Bru?" he asked sweetly. "There are certainly a lot of careless people around these days."

"SHUT UP, YOU OVER-GROWN BAG OF STRIPES!" Bru screamed. "Why don't you get out of here before I paint you with purple polka dots."

"Hmmm, you really should learn to control your anger, Bru," said PJ. "It might get you into trouble, you know."

"GET OUT OF HERE!" Bru shouted.

PJ felt sorry for Bru, but he knew this was not the time to

give him a sermon on controlling anger. So he quietly left and went home. But he had just left when McWhiskers came along.

"Nice day, Bru!" said Mc-Whiskers. He didn't know, of course, that it had not been a nice day at all for Bru.

"It's a lousy day, and I don't need you around to tell me what a nice day it should be," Bru shouted at McWhiskers. "NOW GET OUT OF HERE! GO FIND SOME NICE CAT TO CHASE YOU."

"Bad day, huh?" said Mc-Whiskers. "We all have them. But you must learn to control your anger, Bru. It might get you into trouble, you know."

That was the third time Bru had heard that, and it made him more angry than ever. You could almost see the red come to his face.

"I don't need some shrimpy little pip-squeak like you telling me to control my anger," Bru shouted. He was really getting nasty. "You're nothing but a scrawny little rat, and I hope some nice hungry cat catches you and has a great lunch."

McWhiskers had never heard Bru say something that mean before. "I...I know you don't mean that," said McWhiskers.

Bru could see how hurt his little friend was. But his anger still was like a boiling pot of water.

"I'll even help find the cat!" shouted Bru. "Here kitty, kitty, kitty."

McWhiskers stared at Bru. He was terribly hurt that his friend would say that.

"Well, Bru, it's been nice being your friend," said McWhiskers. "But I can't be your friend any more if you want a cat to eat me. Good-bye, old friend."

Bru could see the tears running down McWhiskers's cheeks. He watched his friend walk sadly down the path. Bru felt sad and hurt that he had let his anger boil over like that. Of course, he did not want to say such a terrible thing to his friend. Of course, he did not want a cat to eat him. Suddenly Bru's anger was gone. Now he had tears running down his cheeks.

Bru ran after McWhiskers. "Stop! Stop!" he shouted. "You know I didn't mean to say such a terrible thing. Please forgive me."

McWhiskers dried his tears. Then Bru gave him a big bear hug. "You're right," said Bru. "I must learn to control my anger. I almost lost one of my best friends."

The next time you get more angry than you should, remember Bru. You don't want to be a grouchy, angry old bear, do you?

Apples for Sale

A Story About Cheating

"**A**PPLES FOR SALE! APPLES FOR SALE!" Fox shouted as he came down the lane.

"What kind are they?" asked Puddles.

"Big red juicy ones," said Fox. He licked his tongue over his lips to emphasize *juicy*.

"Oh, my favorite," said Puddles. "What can I trade you for them?"

"What do you have?" asked Fox.

"I have a bushel of big yel- low juicy apples in a sack," said Puddles. "Here, look at them."

"Don't forget me," said KaWally. "I have a bushel of big juicy pears in a sack."

"Ahhh, you're such lucky creatures," said Fox slyly. "We can work out a trade that you'll never forget. You'll wake up in the middle of the night thinking about me."

"You must be a very good, honest fox," said Puddles. "I'm sure we will be very happy with the trade."

"OK, here's what we do," said Fox. "You'll love this. Bear, put ten of your pears in Hippo's sack while Hippo puts ten of his apples in your sack. That's an even trade. Now to show you how good I am, I will put ten of my red juicy apples in each of your sacks."

"You really are a generous fox," said Puddles. "How thoughtful of you."

"I told you so," said Fox. "Now, just to show you how *super* generous I am, I will give you my last two red apples, pick up my sacks, and go."

Fox gave one big red apple to Puddles and one to KaWally. While they were looking at their big red juicy apples and saying again how generous Fox is, Fox picked up both sacks and walked down the path. Of course, he had all of KaWally's pears, all of Puddles's yellow apples, plus all of the red apples he had put into the sacks.

Fox was almost out of sight when KaWally suddenly realized what had happened. "HE STOLE ALL OUR PEARS AND APPLES!" KaWally shouted.

"What are you talking about?" said Puddles. "Look at the nice red apple he gave us."

"While he took all our apples and pears!" said KaWally.

Sometimes it takes Puddles a little longer to realize what has happened. But when Puddles looked down and saw that his sack was gone, he knew that Fox had cheated him.

"LET'S GO GET HIM!" shouted Puddles.

Puddles and KaWally ran down the path as fast as they could go. They would never have caught Fox except that Fox had been greedy again. He had met Bru with some honey pots and had tried to cheat Bru.

Bru was giving Fox his two honey pots when KaWally and Puddles ran up.

"STOP THAT THIEF!" shouted KaWally.

"HE CHEATED US," shouted Puddles. "He's probably cheating you, too, Bru."

Suddenly Bru realized what he was doing. He was giving his honey pots to Fox and was getting nothing back.

Fox started to run. But he was so greedy that he tried to carry both bags of apples and pears with him. Of course, he couldn't run fast with the two

bags, and so Bru tackled him.

"Trying to cheat my little buddies and me," Bru growled. "Do you know what we do with cheaters around here?"

Bru had his big hand around Fox's throat and was shouting so loud in his face that Fox began to tremble.

"I...I was just leaving," said Fox. "Here, take all of my apples and pears. You can even take my two honey pots. I'm going."

Fox left everything behind and started to run down the lane. But Puddles tackled him this time. "Now what?" asked Fox. "I'm leaving as fast as I can."

"That's fine," said Puddles. "But don't leave your red apples with us. We didn't pay anything for them, and so we don't want

them. Pick up
everything that's
yours and take it
with you."

"Yeah," said
KaWally. "If we get some
of your stuff without
paying for it, we're
cheating, too."

So Fox learned
two good lessons that
day. He learned that he
must never try to cheat Bru
and his friends. And
he learned that they
would never try to
cheat him. Those are
two good lessons for
each of us to learn
today, aren't they?
Please remember that
the next time you eat an
apple or a pear. OK?

Bru's Barrels

A Story About Being Stubborn

"**W**hatcha doing, Bru?" asked KaWally.

"Can't you see that I'm trying to pick some apples?" Bru answered.

KaWally stared at Bru. Yes, he could see that. But it was the way Bru was picking apples that he could not understand. Instead of propping a ladder in the apple tree, Bru had piled some old barrels into a wobbly pile and was standing on top of them to pick apples.

"Your barrels aren't piled very well," said KaWally. "You're going to fall if you don't fix them. I'm sure you know that."

"Are you criticizing a friend?" Bru grumbled. "Are you telling me that I did a poor job of piling these barrels?"

KaWally twitched his nose. He didn't want to criticize his friend. But he could see that the middle barrel was only half on the bottom barrel and the top barrel was not much better. In fact, he was quite amazed that Bru was able to keep his balance on top of this mess.

"Sorry, old buddy," said KaWally. "I just don't want to see you fall and get hurt. You really should get down and fix those barrels so that you don't get hurt."

"I'm not going to get down just because *you* want me to," said Bru. "The barrels are just fine. I did a great job with them."

So rather than talk about the barrels any more, KaWally quietly sat down on an old log to watch Bru. He wanted to see how long it would be before Bru would come tumbling down. He could see that Bru was being very stubborn about the barrels, and it was obvious they were about to fall.

Before long PJ came by. "Whatcha doing, Bru?" he asked.

"What's the matter with all you dumb guys?" Bru yelled. "Can't you see that I'm picking apples?"

"Sure, I can see that," said PJ. "But you usually put a ladder in the tree instead of all those wobbly old barrels."

"I suppose you're telling me that I didn't do a good job stacking these barrels?" Bru shouted at PJ.

"I wasn't going to say that," said PJ. "But now that you mention it, they look like they're going to fall down. You should get down and fix them."

"Stop criticizing my work," said Bru. "I'm not going to get down just because *you* want me to."

PJ shook his head. He didn't want to criticize a friend, but he could see that his friend was being very stubborn. Bru had not done a good job stacking the barrels, and it was obvious they were about to fall. So PJ sat with his friend KaWally on the log to watch Bru tumble.

"I'll give him three more

apples before he falls," KaWally whispered to PJ.

"Five at the most," PJ whis-

pered back.

"Stop whispering about me," Bru yelled. "I'm sure you're criticizing my work. I'm not going to get down and fix these old barrels just because *you* want me to."

Just then McWhiskers came by. He looked at Bru and then at the barrels.

"Bru, you'd better get down and fix those barrels or you're going to have a bad tumble," he said. McWhiskers sometimes didn't mess around. He just said what he thought.

"Go sit on the log with your other big-mouthed friends," Bru shouted. "I'm not going to fix those barrels just because *you* want me to."

"Great idea!" said

McWhiskers. "This is going to be a good show. We could sell tickets to your great tumbling act that is about to happen."

Bru growled and went back to work picking apples. He almost had a bagful. But then it happened. Every time Bru had moved, the wobbly barrels had become even more wobbly. Suddenly the middle barrel slid off the bottom barrel, which made the top barrel tilt to the side, which caused Bru to come tumbling down.

"Five apples," KaWally whispered to PJ. "You win!"

"Stubborn guy, isn't he?" whispered McWhiskers. "Should we help him up?"

"Not yet," said KaWally. "I don't think the show is over yet. Look!"

Bru's apple bag had rolled down the steep hillside, and all his apples had rolled out of the bag. Fox was there, picking them up.

"GET AWAY FROM MY APPLES!" Bru shouted. Then he began rolling all his barrels down the hill at Fox.

"Great show!" said PJ.

"Best in town," said KaWally.

"I'd feel sorry for Bru if he hadn't been so stubborn," said McWhiskers. "But he could have saved himself all this trouble if he had just listened to his friends."

By this time, Fox was gone with all of Bru's apples. And Bru's barrels were gone, too. A very sorry Bru stood by the apple tree.

"I was very stubborn," Bru said to his friends. "I'm sorry. Will you help me prop my ladder in the tree the way I should have done so I can pick the rest of my apples?" Of course, Bru's friends were very happy to help their friend prop his ladder in the apple tree. And they even helped him pick the rest of his apples.

You're never stubborn, are you? If you are, I'm sure you'll remember Bru's barrels.

Ring Those Bells!

A Story About Working Together

"**W**hat are all those things?" Tux asked McWhiskers.

"Bells," said McWhiskers. "But they are not just any old bells. They are handbells. We can have a handbell choir here."

"What is a handbell choir?" KaWally asked.

"We learn to ring the bells together at the right time and make beautiful music," said McWhiskers.

"Like this?" asked Bru. He grabbed two of the biggest bells and began to shake them as fast and as loud as he could.

"No, no, no!" said McWhiskers. "Not like that. I will show you how to do it."

McWhiskers lined up the bells from smallest to largest. Then he lined up his friends from smallest to largest.

Guess who will ring the smallest bells?

Guess who will

ring the largest bells?

You should have seen this lineup of bell ringers. You would want to laugh at them. But, of course, you would be too polite to do that, wouldn't you?

"Ready now?" asked Bru. He grabbed the two nearest bells and began to shake them as hard as he could.

"NO, NO, NO!" shouted McWhiskers. "We must ring these bells together to make beautiful music."

"I thought that was beautiful music," said Bru.

McWhiskers explained again just how the bells could be played to make beautiful music, but Bru wasn't listening. Bru was thinking how he should play the *biggest* bell since he was the biggest.

Bru picked up

the biggest bell to give it one quick bong, but as he lifted the big bell he slipped and fell and the bell landed right over his head!

Everyone laughed. You should have seen it. He really looked funny.

McWhiskers just shook his head. He wondered how he could ever teach this clumsy, show-off bear to make real music.

"Let's try again. We'll start with something simple, like 'Mary Had a Little Lamb,'" said McWhiskers. "When I point to a bell, the person nearest that bell will pick it up and ring it. OK, let's go."

McWhiskers pointed to a bell. Tux and KaWally both reached for it. "Hey! That's mine!" said Tux.

"No way!" said KaWally.

Tux and KaWally began to argue about the bell.

"Stop, stop, stop!" said McWhiskers. "This is no way to make music. The bell is in front of KaWally, so, KaWally, you should pick it up. Ring it just once. Ding. Like that. Tux, you will get a turn later."

KaWally did just what Mc-Whiskers said. So McWhiskers pointed to the next bell. It was PJ's bell this time.

PJ picked up the bell and gave it one nice ding.

"Hey, when is my turn?" asked Bru.

"Shhh, it's coming," said McWhiskers. "Now!"

McWhiskers pointed to the bell. Bru picked it up and shook it.

"No, no, no!" said McWhiskers. "Just one ding. Try it again."

Bru growled. He wanted to do it his way, not a mouse's way. But he picked it up and gave it one nice ding.

McWhiskers went through all of "Mary Had a Little Lamb" with his friends, but it took so long that no one knew what it was.

"Let's do it again," said McWhiskers. "This time we'll do it faster so we can hear the music."

Everything went well until it was Bru's turn. He forgot and shook the bell again.

"No, no, no!" said McWhiskers.

"Let's start over again."

This time Bru remembered. He didn't like to stop with one little ding, but he did it. But things went so slow that no one could tell yet that it was "Mary Had a Little Lamb."

"Once more," said McWhiskers. "This time, Bru, remember to ding the bell, not to shake it. OK, let's go."

This time everything went just right.

"Hey!" said Bru. "Did you hear that? We just played 'Mary Had a Little Lamb'!"

"Can you play that all by yourself, Bru?" McWhiskers asked.

"Sure, I can do anything," said Bru.

But, of course, when Bru tried to play "Mary Had a Little Lamb" all by himself, it sounded terrible.

"It sounds much better when we do it together," said Bru.

If you could have been with McWhiskers and his friends that afternoon, you would be tired of hearing "Mary Had a Little Lamb." They must have played it two dozen times. More than anyone else, Bru wanted to keep playing. He thought it was the most beautiful music he had ever heard.

"Sounds much better when we do it together," Bru said again and again.

That's the way it is with many things we do. We do them better when we do them together. If you don't think so, ask Bru. He will tell you!

A Bicycle for Us All

A Story About Sharing

"**W**hat do you want for your birthday?" Tux asked his friend McWhiskers.

"A bicycle," said McWhiskers. "I have always wanted a bicycle."

"Just for yourself?" asked Tux. "I thought you were my good friend. You can get a bicycle built for two, you know. Then you and I can ride together."

McWhiskers thought that was a great idea. It seemed a great

idea until he realized that this would be a bicycle built for two. Every time he wanted to ride his bike, someone else would need to ride with him.

"I...I really just want a little bike that I can ride," said Mc-Whiskers.

"What did I hear about a birthday bicycle?" KaWally asked. McWhiskers and Tux had not heard him come up.

"McWhiskers wants a bike for his birthday," said Tux. "But he wants a little bike just for himself. I don't think that's fair. Why doesn't he get a bicycle built for two so I can ride with him?"

"But why for two?" asked KaWally. "I want to ride, too. He should get a bicycle built for *three* so I can ride with the two of you."

McWhiskers thought about a bicycle built for three. Every time he wanted to ride his bike, two other people would need to ride with him.

"I...I really just want a little bike that I can ride," said McWhiskers.

"What did I hear about a birthday bicycle?" PJ asked. McWhiskers, Tux, and KaWally had not heard him come up.

"McWhiskers wants a bike for his birthday," said Tux. "But he wants a little bike just for himself. I don't think that's fair. Why doesn't he get a bicycle built for two so I can ride with him?"

"But that's not fair either," said KaWally. "Why doesn't he get a bicycle built for three so I can ride with the two of you?"

"And that's not fair either," said PJ. "Why doesn't he get a bicycle built for *four* so I can ride with the three of you?"

McWhiskers thought about a bicycle built for four. Every time he wanted to ride, he would need to find three others to ride with him.

"I...I really just want a little bike that I can ride," said

McWhiskers quietly.

"What did I hear about a birthday bicycle?" Bru asked. McWhiskers, Tux, KaWally, and PJ had not heard him come up.

"McWhiskers wants a bike for his birthday," said Tux. "But he wants a little bike just for himself. I don't think that's fair. Why doesn't he get a bicycle built for two so I can ride with him?"

"But that's not fair either," said KaWally. "Why doesn't he get a bicycle built for three so I can ride with the two of you?"

"And that's not fair either," said PJ. "Why doesn't he get a bicycle built for four so I can ride with the three of you?"

"Hey, how about me?" asked Bru. "I think he should get a bicycle built for *five* so I can ride with the four of you."

"What's the matter with you all?" asked Puddles. "Don't you want me? How about a bicycle built for *six* so I can ride with the five of you?"

McWhiskers thought about the bicycle built for six. Every time he wanted to ride he would have to find five others to ride with him.

"I...I really just want a little bike that I can ride," said Mc-Whiskers.

"You *do*?" all five of McWhiskers's friends asked. "Well, why didn't you say so?" When they said that, Puddles went behind a big bush and brought the cutest little bike out for McWhiskers.

"It's your birthday gift from the five of us," he said. "We were just kidding about a bicycle built for two, three, four, five, or six."

I suppose McWhiskers was about the happiest birthday mouse you have ever seen. Of course, you may not have seen too many birthday mice, especially birthday mice riding a cute bicycle built for one birthday mouse. But you would love to see McWhiskers riding his little birthday bicycle built for one up and down the path. If you watch carefully, you might see him. OK?

McWhiskers's Pet Cat

A Story About Doing Good to Those Who Hurt Us

"What kind of pet would you like?" Tux asked his friend Bru one day.

Bru thought for a moment. "I'd like a bear hunter for a pet," said Bru. "Bear hunters are always hunting bears. They like to shoot bears or make rugs from our skins. Some-times they even like to hang our heads on their walls."

"But why would you want a bear hunter for a pet?" asked Tux.

"I'd make the bear hunter run across the floor and get my shoes for me," he said. "I'd make him go out into the

woods and find berries for me to eat. If he didn't do what I say, I'd probably make a rug from his skin or hang his head on the wall."

Tux gulped. "You don't want a pet bear hunter," he said. "You want to get even!"

"Could be," said Bru. "But that's what I'd like."

"What about you?" Tux asked PJ. "What would you

like for a pet?"

PJ thought for a moment. "I'd like a zookeeper for a pet," said PJ. "Zookeepers like to keep zebras in zoos."

"But why would you want a zookeeper for a pet? asked Tux. What fun would that be?"

"I'd keep the zookeeper in a cage and feed him bales of straw," said PJ.

Tux gulped. "You don't want a pet zookeeper," he said. "You want to get even!"

"Could be," said PJ. "But that's what I'd like."

Tux was getting a little worried now. His friends all seemed to want to get even with someone for some-thing. "What about you?" Tux asked Puddles. "What would you like for a pet?"

Puddles thought for a moment. "I'd like the artist who draws my picture for my pet," said Puddles. "My artist has made me blue. Anyone knows that hippos are not blue. Hippos are hippo colored. And anyone knows

that hippos walk on four feet, not their back two feet. If I had my artist for a pet, I would

paint
him
with
blue
paint
and
make
him
walk
on all
fours
instead
of his
back two
feet. That's
what I would
make my new
pet do."

Tux gulped.

"You don't want a pet artist," he said. "You want to get even."

"Could be," said Puddles. "But that's what I'd like."

Now Tux really was getting worried about his friends. Did all of his friends just want to get even with someone?

Just then Tux's friend Mc-Whiskers came along. "Hi, Tux!" said McWhiskers. "What's up? What are you doing?"

Tux was almost afraid to ask McWhiskers about a pet. He thought he knew what McWhiskers would answer. But he thought he would ask McWhiskers anyway.

"What would you like for a pet, McWhiskers?" he asked.

"A cat!" said McWhiskers.

"That's what I thought you would say," Tux said sadly. "But why would you want a cat for a pet? Aren't you afraid of cats?"

Tux was almost sure he knew what McWhiskers would

say. He would make that cat miserable because cats catch mice and eat them. He might even want to catch the cat and eat it. That made Tux shake a little.

"Why would I want a cat for a pet?" McWhiskers answered. Then he thought for a moment. "I would be kind to my pet cat," he said. "I would pet it and make it purr. I would feed it and take good care of it."

Tux was surprised. He could hardly believe what he was hearing.

"But why would you do that?" he asked "I thought you did not like cats because they catch mice and eat them."

"That's true," said McWhiskers. "But we must do good to those who hurt us. If a mouse is kind to a cat, who knows?

We might help cats everywhere to learn to be kind to mice everywhere. Wouldn't that be special?"

"Do good to those who hurt

you?" asked Tux. "That's special, isn't it? McWhiskers, I think you have the right idea."

"I think so, too," said McWhiskers.

Do you think so, too? Do you think Jesus would be pleased if you are kind to those who hurt you?

Why Am I Blue?

A Story About Being Content with What We Have or What We Are

"**B**lue!" said Puddles. "Why did I have to be blue? Who ever heard of a blue hippo?"

"So what would you like to be?" asked McWhiskers.

"Look at all these beautiful colors," said Puddles. He held up a fistful of crayons. "Look! Yellow, orange, green, purple, red, pink. Beautiful colors. So why do I have to be blue?"

"I should complain, too!" said McWhiskers. "I'm gray. Why

couldn't I be another color? I'm not even sure that gray is a color!"

"Why not?" asked Puddles. "Let's pretend that we are different colors. We may see something else we like better."

Puddles looked through his fistful of crayons. "Here," he said. "I'll be red, and you be green."

As soon as he said that,

Puddles was a pretend red. McWhiskers was a pretend green. Both Puddles and McWhiskers almost jumped from their skins when they saw the pretend red and pretend green.

"*Yuck!*" said Puddles.

"*Terrible!*" said McWhiskers.

That ended the pretend red and green. Puddles was just plain blue again, and McWhiskers was just plain gray.

"OK, those were the wrong colors," said Puddles. "Let's try again." Puddles held up his fistful of crayons and looked through them.

"Here we go!" he said.

"I'll be a pretend yellow, and you be a pretend pink."

As soon as he said that, Puddles was a pretend yellow, and McWhiskers was a pretend pink. But Puddles and McWhiskers almost jumped from their skins again when they saw the pretend yellow and pink.

"*Yuck!*" said McWhiskers.

"*Terrible!*" said Puddles.

That ended the pretend yellow and pink. Puddles was just plain blue again, and McWhiskers was just plain gray.

"Those were certainly the wrong colors," said Puddles. "Once more!"

Puddles held up his fistful of crayons and looked through them.

"We haven't tried orange or purple," he said.

"OK, you be purple, and I'll be orange."

As soon as he said that, Puddles was a pretend orange, and McWhiskers was a pre-

tend purple. But the two of them almost jumped from their skins when they saw the pretend colors.

"*Yuck!*" they both said this time.

"There must be an answer," said Puddles. "Just one more time!"

Puddles held up his fistful of crayons. "Aha!" he said. "This time I have it. You'll be red with green polka dots, and I'll be yellow with purple stripes."

McWhiskers was almost ready to say *yuck* before he saw the pretend colors. But he thought it would be polite to see them anyway.

As soon as Puddles said that, he was a pretend yellow with purple stripes, and McWhiskers was a

pretend red with green polka dots.

But when they both saw

these terrible colors, they screamed.

"GET THIS OFF ME," shouted McWhiskers.

"ME, TOO!" shouted Puddles.

As soon as he said that, he was just plain Puddles blue, and McWhiskers was just plain McWhiskers gray.

"You know," said Puddles. "I'm beginning to like my blue much better."

"I've always liked my nice soft gray," said McWhiskers. "We should learn to like the way we were made because we can't change it."

"That's what I think, too," said Puddles. "Who ever wanted to change our colors anyway?"

I hope you're glad that God made you the way He did. If you are, thank Him. If you aren't, ask Him to help you learn to like it better each day.

The Flying Bear

A Story About Being Content with Who You Are and What You Can Do

"Did you hear about Bru?" KaWally asked McWhiskers.

"I heard that he's going to fly," said McWhiskers. "Is that what you mean?"

"Yes, but he can't, can he?" asked KaWally.

"A bear, fly?" said McWhiskers. "I've never seen a bear fly, have you?"

"No, but suppose Bru has found something special," he said. "Suppose he's grown wings or something like that."

Seeing Bru with wings was too much for McWhiskers. He burst out laughing.

"Well, we'd best get over to the meadow and see what Bru's planning to do," said McWhiskers.

KaWally and McWhiskers hurried over to the meadow. On the way they saw Puddles

and PJ. They, too, had heard the news.

"Bru's going to fly!" said Puddles. "He asked us all to come to see him do it."

"You mean Bru's going to *try* to fly," said McWhiskers. "There's a big difference, you know."

"But he didn't say that," said Puddles. "He said he's going to fly."

McWhiskers did not want to argue with Puddles. So he kept quiet.

When the friends reached the meadow, they saw Bru, stacking some old crates. He was just putting the last crate in place at the top of the stack.

"Glad to see you," said Bru. "You are about to witness something wonderful today, a flying bear."

"I told you he's going to fly," Puddles whispered to McWhiskers.

McWhiskers looked at Bru. "You can't fly with a bunch of old crates," he said. "Did you grow some wings?"

"I didn't grow them, my friend," said Bru. "I made them."

For the first time McWhiskers and his friends saw some strange wings lying on the ground. Bru had tied some old sacks onto some long poles to make the wings.

"Now you guys are going to tie my wings onto my arms," said Bru. "Then I'm ready."

I know you would have laughed at the sight. It really did look funny to see those friends tying the crude wings onto a bear.

"You're not really going to try this, are you, Bru?" asked

McWhiskers. "You might get hurt, you know."

"No, I'm not going to try it," said Bru. "I'm going to *do* it. I'm going to fly. You will now watch the first flying bear go soaring out over the valley. You won't laugh then."

"But why?" asked Puddles. "I don't want to fly. Mc-Whiskers or PJ or Tux or KaWally doesn't want to fly. Why do you suddenly want to fly?"

"Owl can fly," said Bru. "He's nothing but

a scrawny little bird. If he can fly, I can fly."

"But God made him with wings," McWhiskers argued. "He made Owl so he could fly. He didn't make you with wings so you could fly."

"So I've made my own wings," said Bru. "Here we go!"

Bru climbed to the top of the old crates. He spread his wings and began to flap them. But nothing happened.

Bru flapped his wings faster. Still nothing happened.

"Maybe you need feathers," said Puddles.

"Don't be funny," said Bru. "Maybe I need to soar."

As soon as he said that, Bru took a leap from the crates and began flapping his wings as fast as he could. Puddles almost expected to see Bru fly out across the valley. Instead, Bru

came down with a horrible crash. The crates tumbled on top of him. His wings crumpled into a dozen pieces.

"Ow! Ow! Ow!" Bru complained as he lay in the dust.

Just then Owl came flying in to see his friends. He soared in a wide circle, then landed gracefully on a stack of crates.

"I just heard the news," said Owl. "Bru is going to fly. May I watch?"

"No, I am not going to fly," said Bru. "I can't fly. I just tried. It was terrible. But how does a scrawny little bird like you do it? I thought if you could do it, I could do it."

"Gracious," said Owl. "I can't do all the wonderful things you can do. Why must you also try to do the one thing I *can* do?"

"I told him God made you

that way," said McWhiskers. "I guess God made Bru to do a lot of wonderful things that only bears can do."

"So I'd better do what bears do best," said Bru. "Then Owl can do what owls do best."

"That's probably a good idea for all of us to remember," said McWhiskers. It's a good idea for you to remember, too. If you do, you will do what you do best and let others do what they do best. If you do, you'll be much happier!

Too Much Fun Food

A Story About Eating Too Much Sweet Stuff

"GUESS WHAT?" Puddles shouted to his friends. "There's a carnival in town. We can get lots of people food there, especially the sweet stuff they talk about."

"Hmmmp," said Bru. "I suppose the people there will capture us and put us in cages so they can stare at us and call us animals."

"Oh, come on, Bru, be a good sport," said McWhiskers. "I've always wanted to go to a carnival. I've always wanted to have some people food. Let's go."

Bru grumbled and grouched a little more, but at last he agreed to go to the carnival. "I guess it's OK," said Bru.

Puddles and Bru and their friends did not want to try any of the rides at the carnival. They wanted to taste the people food, especially the sweet stuff.

First, they had the biggest ice cream cones you have ever seen. They had never had ice cream before. Bru thought it tasted like honey. McWhiskers thought it tasted like cheese, only better. Everyone liked the ice cream cones so well that he wanted another. Then each wanted another and another and another. Nobody knows how many ice cream cones each one had.

"We'd better be careful," said KaWally. "We might get sick."

"From that wonderful stuff?" said Bru. "No way!"

Next, Bru and his friends tasted some cotton candy. They had never eaten cotton candy before. It was so sweet and good. One was certainly not enough. Actually, three were not enough. Before long, Bru and his friends had eaten more cotton candy than you

would think of eating.

"We'd better be careful," said Tux. "We might get sick."

"Get sick?" said Puddles. "No way! We never get sick."

Next was the lemonade. Bru thought this tasted like honey, too. McWhiskers even talked himself into thinking it tasted like cheese. Of course, you know that lemonade really doesn't taste like cheese. But when you are enjoying something, you can think lots of good thoughts about it, can't you?

No one knows how much lemonade Bru and his friends drank. You really don't want to know, do you? But it was much more than any bear, or boy or girl, should drink.

Bru and Puddles and friends were headed to-

ward the hot dog stand when
Bru rubbed his tummy. "I...I
don't feel so good," he said.
     "Me neither," said Puddles.
     McWhiskers
tried to
squeak

out a "me neither," but he
could hardly do that. Tux and
KaWally had
yucky looks

on their faces, and PJ was already sitting down.

"I...I think we must have eaten too much," said Puddles. "I really am sick."

"Me, too," said McWhiskers.

"Urk," said KaWally.

"I...I think we should go home," said Tux.

So Puddles and Bru and their friends waddled home. Later, one of them would sometimes say they got sick because they ate people food. But most of the time they all realized that they ate too much sweet stuff, like ice cream and cotton candy and lemonade.

You would never eat too many sweets, of course. Would you? The next time you are tempted to eat too much sweet stuff, remember Puddles and Bru and their friends.

133

Being Good or Doing Good?

A Story About Doing Good Things

"What are you doing, Puddles?" asked KaWally.

Puddles was sitting like a statue on an old stump, with his head resting on one hand. KaWally could see that he was doing noth- ing, but he thought he should ask what he was doing because that was the polite thing to say to someone who was doing nothing.

"I'm being good," said Puddles.

"By sitting there, doing nothing?" asked KaWally.

"Yes," said Puddles. "I heard that I'm being good whenever I'm not doing something bad. So if I sit here doing nothing, I'm not doing anything bad."

KaWally thought about that a while. "So if you aren't doing something bad, you are doing something good?" he asked.

"That's what I heard," said Puddles.

"I don't think that's right," said KaWally. "I think you're *being* good when you're *doing* good."

"Huh?" Puddles asked. This was a little hard for Puddles to understand.

"Come with me," said KaWally. "Let's try something."

Puddles jumped down from the big stump and went with his friend KaWally. They walked down the path until they came to PJ, who had a big bale of straw in his wheelbarrow.

"Morning, PJ," said Puddles. "Do you need some help?"

"Oh, yes, please," said PJ. "I need a big strong friend to help me carry this big bale of straw."

Puddles helped PJ lift the big bale of straw and carry it where PJ wanted it.

"How can I ever thank you?" said PJ. "I didn't know how I was going to do that alone. But you came at just the right time. Thank you. You are a *good* helper, Puddles. You really are a *good* guy!"

"Are you saying he was *being* good to you because he was *doing* something good for you?" KaWally asked PJ.

"Yes, I am," said PJ. "Puddles did something good for me. So I think he was *being* good to me."

KaWally looked at Puddles. Puddles looked at KaWally. Now Puddles was beginning to understand what KaWally had said. Doing good things for someone is being good to that person. He would not have been good to PJ if he had just sat on a stump, doing nothing.

Farther down the path the

two friends met McWhis- kers. He was huffing and puffing, trying to move a big tree branch.

"Need some help?" Puddles asked.

"Oh, am I glad to see you, my big friend," said McWhiskers. "This big branch fell over my path, and I've been working all morning trying to move it."

"Here, let me do it for you," said Puddles.

Puddles reached down, picked up the big branch, and carried it out in the woods. "There, anything for a friend," said Puddles.

"You are a *good* friend," said McWhiskers.

"Are you saying he was *being* good to you because he was *doing* something good for you?" asked KaWally.

"Yes, that's exactly what I'm saying," said McWhiskers. "He was *being* good to me because he *did* something good for me."

"I understand," said

That's a good thing to remember, isn't it? You will want to do good things for others.

Puddles. "I can't *be* good to you by sitting on a stump, doing nothing. If I'm going to be good to my friends, I must get off the stump and do good things for them."

When you do, people will say you are *being* good to them. But they won't say that if you just sit on a stump, doing nothing.

The Old Hat

A Story About Not Judging Others

"Look what I found!" said Bru.

Bru's friends—Tux, KaWally, McWhiskers, and PJ— gathered around to see what he had found. They knew it must be something strange for Bru to shout the way he did.

"It's nothing but an old hat," said Tux. "What's so exciting about that?"

"It's not just any old hat," said Bru. "Look closely."

Bru's friends came in closer to look.

"It still just looks like an old hat," said Tux. "What's the problem, Bru?"

"What's the problem? I'll tell you what's the problem," said Bru. "Some stranger wore this old hat here to our community. He's a suspicious fellow. You can tell by looking at the hat. I tell you, whoever wore this hat is no good."

"How can you tell?" asked KaWally.

"Look!" said Bru. "Look at the color of the hat. It's dark green. Do you know what that means?"

All of Bru's friends shook

their heads. They did not know what it meant.

"I'll tell you," said Bru. "Anyone who wears a dark green hat is no good. My daddy told me that. He's probably a bear hunter. He's probably hiding behind a bush, waiting until the rest of you leave. Then, BAM! The next time you see me, I'll be nothing but a rug in that guy's house. That's what it means."

Bru's friends looked surprised. They

had never heard that about dark green hats before.

"Furthermore," said Bru, "whoever wore this hat has bad character."

"How can you tell that?" asked PJ.

"How can I tell that?" Bru repeated. "I'll tell you. Do you see how rumpled this old hat is? It looks beat up. The guy who wore this hat has a personality problem. He's mean and selfish. He wants only to please himself. He probably beats his wife and kids. He may even steal from them. You don't want to meet this guy. You won't like him."

"Wow," said PJ. "You must really be smart, Bru, to know all that. What else did you learn from this old hat?"

"What else?" said Bru. "I'll tell you what else. The guy who wore this hat here is a spy. He came here to find out all he can about each one of you. You'll find out when it's dark tonight and he breaks into your homes and steals all you have and beats you up."

Bru's eyes grew dark as he said this. His eyelids fell down over his eyes like dark clouds coming over the sun.

"You'll see . . ." Bru whispered, with a rasping voice.

If you could look at Bru's friends now, you would see their eyes as big as saucers. You might even see the hair standing up on their heads.

"Wow!" was about all Bru's friends could say. What else can you say when a friend knows that much, or thinks he knows that much?

Suddenly Bru grabbed PJ. "Shhh," he said.

"What's the matter?" asked PJ. "You look as if you're afraid of something."

"Shhh," said Bru. "He's over there under that bush. Do you see him? He's a big ugly lump."

Bru's friends looked over at the bush. They did see a big dark shape lying under it. It looked like someone taking a nap. Or maybe someone was there spying.

"He's evil!" whispered Bru. "Look at him! A big hulk, waiting to pounce on us. I say let's all get clubs and beat him to it."

Bru and his friends went into the woods and made big clubs from limbs that had fallen. Quietly, they crept toward the dark shape. When they were almost there, the dark shape moved. Two big arms came up.

"Now!" said Bru. "Rush him! Get him before he gets us." Bru and his friends rushed toward the dark shape. They raised their clubs to beat on him. But just before they reached the dark shape, it got up. It was huge. It was much bigger than they had expected.

"RUN FOR YOUR LIVES!" shouted McWhiskers. "He's much too big for us."

Just then a voice called out from the dark shape. "What are you guys up to?" the voice said. "What are you doing with all those big clubs?"

"PUDDLES!" they all shouted. "What are you doing here?"

"I lost my hat," said Puddles. "I was trying to find it. Then I got tired and decided to take a nap."

"*Your* hat?" asked Bru. "*This* hat?"

"*My* hat," said Puddles. "Oh, thank you, Bru. You found it. This was my father's hat. He was the kindest, most wonderful hippo who ever lived. People always said they could tell how wonderful he was by the hat that he wore. It is so soft and floppy. And the forest green color told people how much he loved the woods."

"Well, Bru, what do you think about that?" McWhiskers asked.

"I...I think I made a terrible

mistake," said Bru. "I think we should never judge someone by the hat he wears."

"Or the clothes she wears, or the house he lives in, or anything else except the person," said Tux.

"That's just what I was going to say," said Bru.

You would never judge someone by the hat or clothes or house or car or anything else that person has, would you? Bru would tell you not to do that. That is, *now* he would tell you not to do it.

The Honey Tree

A Story About the Way God Gives Us Food

"**W**here are you going with that ladder and honey pot, Bru?" Tux asked.

"I'm looking for a honey tree," said Bru. With one hand Bru was carrying a wooden ladder. With the other he was carrying a honey pot.

Tux scratched his head. "A honey tree?" he said. "Do you plant honeycombs so that a honey tree can grow from them?"

Now Bru scratched his head. He had never thought about planting honeycombs to get honey. He had always just found a honey tree and filled his honey pot with honey. Where did the honey at the honey tree come from?

Farther down the path Bru

met KaWally.

"Where are you
going with that
ladder and honey
pot, Bru?" KaWally
asked.

"I'm looking for
a honey tree," said
Bru.

KaWally
scratched his head.

"A honey tree?" he said. "Do you plant bees so that a honey tree can grow from them?"

Now Bru scratched his head again. He had never thought about planting bees to get honey. He had always just found a honey tree and filled his honey pot with honey. Where did the honey at the honey tree come from?

Farther down the path Bru met PJ.

"Where are you going with that ladder and honey pot, Bru?" PJ asked.

"I'm looking for a honey tree," said Bru.

PJ scratched his head. "A honey tree?" he said. "Do you plant honey pots so that a honey tree can grow from them?"

Now Bru scratched his head again. He had never thought about planting honey pots to get honey. He had always just found a honey tree and filled his honey pot with honey. Where did the honey at the honey tree come from?

Before long, Bru found the honey tree. Bees were buzzing in and out of a big hole. Bru could see the honeycomb inside the hole. He would climb up on his ladder and shoo the bees away. Then he would stuff the honey into his honey pot.

But as Bru watched the bees buzzing in and out of the hole, he thought about the questions his friends had asked. Where did the honey in the honey tree come from?

Bru looked at the tree. It didn't look like a honeycomb or a honey pot. It didn't look like a bee. It was just an ordi-

149

nary tree that some bees had found. They had built a honeycomb in the tree.

"But where does the honey come from?" he asked.

"God helps the bees make the honey," a voice said.

There was McWhiskers. "Don't you see the honey up in the honey tree?" asked McWhiskers.

Bru looked up at the honey. He looked at the bees. And he looked at the tree.

"God made the tree where the bees could put their honey," said McWhiskers. "He made the bees so they could make the honey. And He helped them make the honey so you and they can have food to eat."

"Yum-m-m, I'm ready for my part," said Bru. So he started up the ladder with his honey pot, ready to get some honey.

McWhiskers looked at all the bees buzzing around the honeycomb. "I guess God makes bears and mice different, too," he said. "The bees won't hurt Bru. But I'd better get out of here."

God gives your food to you in many different ways. I'm sure you always remember that it came from God. And I'm sure you remember to thank Him for it. Can you think of some of the ways He gives it to you?

151

Someone's in My House

A Story About Helpfulness

"Bru, help me!" said Puddles. "I was just going through my doorway when I heard someone in my house. Come and help me get him out."

Bru raised one sleepy eye and looked at Puddles. "Can't you see I'm taking a nap? Come on, Puddles. A big guy like you can take care of it. Come back after my nap and I'll help you," said Bru.

"After your nap?" Puddles said. "That could be next spring!"

But Bru didn't even hear him. He was fast asleep again.

Puddles looked at Bru sleeping. He was almost angry with Bru, but he really did not have time to be angry. He had to find someone to help him.

"PJ, help me!" Puddles said

when he found his friend. "I was just going through my doorway when I heard some-one in my house. Come and help me get him out."

PJ was fixing a wheel on his wheelbarrow. He hardly looked up at Puddles. "I wish I could, old pal," he said. "But you can see that I'm really busy. Come back tomorrow. Maybe I can help you then."

"TOMORROW?" Puddles shouted. "By tomorrow that thief will have walked off with everything I own. He may even take my house with him."

But Puddles could see that PJ was completely interested in his wheelbarrow. He was almost angry with PJ, but he did not have time to be angry. So he ran to find another friend to help him.

"KaWally, help me!"

Puddles said when he found him.

KaWally had just spread out a picnic lunch of eucalyptus leaves and had a mouth filled with them. He almost half heard Puddles's story about someone in his house.

"Really, Puddles, you *are* interrupting me," he said. "Do you know how hard it is for me to get these wonderful eucalyptus leaves? You wouldn't want to spoil this wonderful lunch I have spread out, would you, old pal? Come back after lunch and I'll be glad to help you."

Puddles looked surprised. That's probably because he was surprised.

"By that time the thief will have taken everything I have and be far away," he said. But KaWally was enjoying his euca-

anyone help him?

Puddles looked for the next biggest friend. When he found Tux, he was surprised to see him sitting on a big cake of ice.

"Tux, help me!" said Puddles. "I was just going through my doorway when I heard some-one in my house. Come and help me get him out."

"Puddles, really!" said Tux. "Do you know what I had to do to get this cake of ice? Who knows how long it will be before I get another one. Come back when it is

lyptus leaves so much that he didn't even hear Puddles.

Puddles sighed. Wouldn't

melted and I'll help you."

Puddles looked at the big cake of ice. "That could be next week!" he said. But Tux was enjoying the cake of ice so much that he didn't even hear Puddles.

Puddles felt sad and hurt. His friends were more interested in naps and wheelbarrows and picnics and ice cakes than they were in helping him. Wouldn't anyone help him?

A big tear trickled down Puddles's cheek. "Won't someone help me?" he cried out.

"I'll help you, old buddy!" a voice said.

"McWhiskers!" said Puddles. "You really will help me? But you're so little."

"I'm big enough to help a friend," said McWhiskers. "What do you need?"

Puddles told McWhiskers about going through his doorway and hearing someone in his house. He told him about his friends and their naps, wheelbarrows, lunches and ice cakes.

"Let's go!" said McWhiskers. He grabbed the little baseball bat he had been playing with, took Puddles by the hand, and raced toward Puddles's house.

It really did look funny, seeing little McWhiskers with his little baseball bat, half dragging big Puddles to his house to fight whoever was there.

"Shhh!" said Puddles when they reached the door. "Better be quiet. He might jump us."

But as soon as they were inside, McWhiskers shouted in a roaring voice that would have frightened even Bru. "WHO'S IN THIS HOUSE? GIVE UP OR I'LL COME AND GET YOU," he shouted.

Puddles was almost afraid of McWhiskers. It seemed that the whole house shook.

"It...it's just me," a trembling voice said.

Puddles and McWhiskers looked at a chair in the corner of the room. They saw Owl perched on the back of the chair next to the table.

"Owl!" they both said. "What are you doing here?"

"I...I came in from the rain this morning," he said. "Is this your house? I'm sorry. I didn't know."

"It's Puddles's house," said McWhiskers softly.

"Then I'd best be going," said Owl. "Sorry to have bothered you."

"No, wait," said Puddles. "Why don't you both stay for an outside picnic lunch? I want to celebrate a very brave McWhiskers who helped me when I

needed a helper."

If you had stopped for lunch that day you would have been surprised to see a mouse, an owl, and a blue hippo laughing and having a great time. And best of all, it was a special lunch to cele-brate the brave mouse who became a good helper for a friend. Of course, you would have done the same, wouldn't you?

The Hollow Log

A Story About Big and Little

"Why are you so sad?" Puddles asked his friend McWhiskers.

"Because you're so big and I'm so little," said McWhiskers. "Everyone thinks you're so important because you're so big. And they think I'm not important because I'm so little."

"But you *are* important, little friend," said Puddles. "I think so."

"See, you even called me *little* friend," said McWhiskers. "You're trying to make me feel better, but deep down you still think I'm just a little guy."

Now Puddles looked sad. He didn't want to hurt his friend McWhiskers. It was true

that McWhiskers was little. But all mice are little. And it was true that Puddles was big. But all hippos are big. So what could Puddles do?

"Why are you both so sad?" Tux asked as he came along.

"McWhiskers is sad because he's so much smaller than I, and I'm sad because he's sad," said Puddles.

"Then I suppose I should be sad because you're both sad," said Tux. "Come on, guys, someone has to make you feel good."

"It's no use, Tux," said McWhiskers. "Big people are just more important than little people."

"So I'm half as important as Puddles and twice as important as you?" asked Tux. "Anyway, we don't have time to talk about this. Bru is crying his heart out. He's really sad. We all need to help him."

So Puddles and McWhiskers forgot about their problems of being big or small and ran with Tux to help Bru. They didn't want Bru to cry.

"What's the matter, Bru?"

McWhiskers asked when he found his friend.

Bru was sitting in the middle of a big hollow log. He was crying big bear tears.

"My gold watch!" he cried. "I was sitting here by this big knothole in the hollow log and accidentally dropped my gold watch in that hole."

"Why don't you just reach in and get it?" asked McWhiskers.

"I've tried a hundred times," said Bru. "But my arm is too big. Tux and KaWally and PJ all tried, too. But their arms are too big. I know Puddles couldn't do it because he's too big. And your arm is too short."

"So why don't you just crawl into the hollow log and get it?" McWhiskers asked.

"I tried a hundred times,"

said Bru. "But I'm too big. Tux and KaWally and PJ all tried. But they're too big, too. There's no way for Puddles to do it. He's much too big."

"So why don't I just crawl into the log and get it for you?" said McWhiskers.

Before anyone could say anything, McWhiskers crawled

into the log and brought Bru's gold watch out to him. Bru was so happy that he hugged McWhiskers.

"MY GOLD WATCH! MY GOLD WATCH!" Bru shouted. "McWhiskers, you're the most important person of us all. Only you could get my gold watch back for me."

Suddenly McWhiskers smiled his biggest smile all day. "Did you guys hear that?" he asked. "Bru said I'm the most important guy of all today. Do you really mean that Bru? Do you really think I'm important, even though I'm the smallest of you all?"

"Of course," said Bru. "You're important today because you *are* the smallest. Only the smallest one could go into the hollow log and get my watch for me."

"So small can be important," said McWhiskers, clapping his hands. "Small can even be more important than big."

Then Bru had an idea. He ran home as fast as he could go. In a few minutes he came back with a big button that said, "Think IMPORTANT." Then he pinned the big button on McWhiskers. It was almost bigger than he was. "That's your hero medal," said Bru. "So even though you're little, think IMPORTANT!"

Sometimes you may think you are smaller or slower or thinner or something less than your friends. When you do, remember McWhiskers and his button. Small may sometimes be IMPORTANT. Small may sometimes be even more important than big.

The Other Guy in the Mirror

A Story About the Way Others Respond to Us

Bru, of course, had never seen a mirror before. That is, he had never seen one before he found one at the dump.

"Look at that picture in the picture frame," said Bru. Actually, Bru was looking at his face in the mirror.

"That is about the ugliest guy I have ever seen," Bru said to himself. "I think I'll have some fun. I'll scare him."

Bru braced himself and let go with a terrific growl. It almost made the forest shake. He watched the other guy in the mirror as he did this. So the other guy in the mirror growled back at Bru as loudly and ferociously as Bru.

Bru wasn't expecting this, and so he looked surprised, perhaps even a little scared. So, of course, the other guy in the mirror looked a little surprised, perhaps even

a little scared.

"So...scared of me, huh?" Bru growled at the other guy in the mirror. Bru bared his big teeth at the other guy. But the other guy bared his teeth just as much at Bru.

"Trying to growl at me, are you?" Bru shouted angrily.

"I'll just stick my tongue out at you to show you what I think of you."

Of course, the other guy in the mirror stuck his tongue out at Bru, just as much as Bru had done to him.

"I don't like you," Bru told the other guy in the mirror. "You're the ugliest guy I've ever seen. And everything I do, you do back at me. I wish I could punch you in the nose."

But how do you punch the other guy in the mirror in the nose? Bru thought that would be too hard, and so he didn't even try it.

Bru lowered his eyelids and gave the other guy in the mirror the meanest look he could give. But the other guy in the mirror gave Bru a look just as mean.

When Bru was giving this meanest look to the other guy in the mirror, KaWally came along.

"Whatcha doing?" KaWally said with a chuckle. "Why such a mean and ugly look?"

"There's some ugly guy in this thing," said Bru. "Every time I frown at him, he frowns at me. When I growl at him, he growls back at me. He does everything back at me. Watch this."

Bru growled the meanest growl he could at the other guy in the mirror. Sure enough, the other guy did the same thing back to Bru.

Bru stuck his tongue out again at the other guy. But the other guy stuck his tongue out at Bru.

Then Bru gave his mean old bear look at the other guy. The other guy gave Bru the same mean old bear look back.

"You're right," said KaWally. "He does everything you do. Everything you do to him, he does back to you."

"I'd like to punch him in the nose," said Bru. "But I don't know how to do that to him."

"I have a better idea," said KaWally. "Why don't you smile at him? Perhaps he will smile back at you."

"Smile at that ugly thing?" said Bru. "Never! I hate that guy."

"I don't know, Bru," said KaWally. "He's just doing what most people do. Have you ever noticed? If you look mean at others, they will usually look mean at you. If you look happy at others, they will look happy back at you. And if you smile at others, they will often smile back at you."

"Really?" asked Bru. "I never thought about that."

"Try it," said KaWally. "See if it works."

"Oh, all right," said Bru. "I don't like that ugly guy, but I'll try smiling at him."

So Bru smiled his sweetest smile at the other guy in the mirror. The other guy smiled his sweetest smile back at Bru.

"So, what do you think?" asked KaWally. "It works, doesn't it?"

"Yeah! It really does," said Bru. Then Bru tried it again. He smiled his sweetest smile at the other guy in the mirror. So the other guy in the mirror smiled his sweetest smile right back at Bru.

"Wow! I kinda like that guy," said Bru. "In fact, he really isn't so ugly. He's even kinda handsome. Don't you think?"

"Of course," said KaWally. "I think he even looks a little like you."

Bru sat down on a big stump. He smiled again. The other guy smiled back. "Nice guy," said Bru. Now Bru was having so much fun that he kept on smiling, laughing, and telling funny stories to the other guy in the mirror. And the other guy in the mirror kept smiling and laughing back at Bru. Bru even thought he was telling funny stories back to him.

So Bru and the guy in the mirror became very good friends. On a nice day you can often see Bru sitting on a big stump, smiling, and saying happy things to his friend in the mirror.

And Bru will tell you that the best part of all is watching his friend smile back at him.

You may want to try this with real people, not the person in the mirror. Smile! See if the person will smile back at you. Bru will tell you that it really works.

Lost in the Forest

A Story About Pride

The moon was rising over the forest, and McWhiskers had still not found the path that led home. He had been looking all afternoon. But it never seemed to be where it should be.

"This is silly," McWhiskers complained to himself. "Mice don't get lost. I'll never tell my friends about this. They'll laugh at me."

But McWhiskers knew that he was lost. Mice don't get lost, but he was lost. He didn't know where to find the path that led home.

McWhiskers sat down beside a big tree. He looked at the moon shining through the leaves. "I wish I were home," he said. "I'm so lonely out here."

Just then McWhiskers heard a rustling noise in the tree above him. What was that? McWhiskers was afraid.

"Who-o-o," said a voice. It was Owl, sitting on a big branch of the tree. "Are you lost?" asked Owl. "If you are, I'll take you to the path that leads home."

McWhiskers wanted to say, "Yes, I am lost." But sud-denly he thought of his friends laughing at him if they heard he had been lost. He was too proud to admit that he was lost.

"N...no, I'm not lost," he said. "I'm just on my way home."

"Oh, sorry to bother you then," said Owl. Off he flew.

McWhiskers almost called after him. But when he opened his mouth, he thought he

could see his friends laughing at him. So he kept quiet.

McWhiskers felt sad and very lonely as he watched Owl fly away. Owl could have taken him to his path, and he would have been on his way home. Why did he tell Owl that he wasn't lost? Why didn't he admit it so he could get home? But McWhiskers knew why. His pride kept him from saying that to Owl. Owl might tell his friends that he had been lost, and they would laugh at him.

McWhiskers went one way for quite some time. But he was sure that was the wrong way. Then he went another way for a long time. But that certainly was not the right way. So he sat down beside a big tree and looked at the moon.

Suddenly McWhiskers heard a noise in the tree above him. What was that? He was afraid.

"It's me again," a voice said. It was Owl. "Are you sure you're not lost?"

McWhiskers almost said, "Yes, help me find the path." But he thought he saw his friends laughing at him, and so he said, "No...no, I'm just taking a walk in the forest."

"In the middle of the night?" asked Owl. "Going this way and that way? Are you sure you don't want me to take you to your path that leads home?"

More than anything in the world right now, McWhiskers wanted to say yes. But he thought he could still see his friends laughing at him, and so he said, "No, thank you."

"OK, I tried," said Owl. "Have a good trip home."

Owl flew off through the

trees. McWhiskers wanted to shout for him to come back. But he didn't. He was too proud to have Owl lead him to the path.

McWhiskers tried a new way. Surely this would lead to his path. But it didn't. Then he tried another new way. But he was sure he was going even farther from home.

At last McWhiskers sat by a big tree. Hot tears ran down his cheeks. He was lost, and he knew it. He had wandered around the forest all night. It was almost morning.

"I wish Owl would come back!" McWhiskers said. "I'd tell him I'm lost, and I would ask him to help me find my path."

"Someone mention my name?" a voice said.

"Owl! It's you!" said Mc-Whiskers. "Oh, please lead me to my path. I'm really lost and want to go home."

"I knew you were lost," said Owl. "So I've been hanging around all night, watching you. Do you see that big tree over there? Your path is just on the other side of it."

McWhiskers almost ran to the big tree. And when he found his path on the other side of it, he started to run home. Then he stopped. He saw Owl, making sure he was going the right way.

"Thank you, Owl," said McWhiskers. "If I can ever help you, let me know."

"Have a good nap when you get home!" Owl called back.

You can be sure that Mc-Whiskers had a long nap when he got home. You can also be sure that home looked better than it had ever looked to him.

Owl kept McWhiskers's secret. So his friends never laughed about McWhiskers getting lost. I know you will keep his secret, too, won't you?

Dozens of Honey Pots

A Story About Deceiving Others

"What is Bru doing?" PJ asked his friends. "He's sneaking around like he's hiding something."

"You're right," said Tux. "Every time I see him, he has a honey pot under his arm. Then he looks at me with a silly grin."

"And he acts as if he is trying to hide the honey pot," said KaWally.

"He's up to something," said McWhiskers. "I think we should find out what it is."

"But I suppose he can carry honey pots around if he wants to," said KaWally.

"That's right," said Puddles. "But it isn't right to hide something from us. There's no doubt about it. Bru is trying to deceive us all."

"Shhh, I hear him coming," said Tux. "Let's hide behind this bush until he's even with us. Then let's step out and surprise him."

Bru's friends hid behind a big bush as he came along the path, whistling. When Bru came near the bush, they all stepped out.

"Surprise!" they said together.

Sure enough, Bru had a honey pot. He grinned a silly grin and said, "Hi."

"What are

you doing, Bru?" asked KaWally. "What are you up to?"

"Up to?" asked Bru. His grin looked even sillier now. "Up to? Why do you think I'm up to something?"

"Come on, Bru," said Mc-Whiskers. "We're not dumb, you know. You're trying to deceive us. We can tell."

"Aw, you guys know I would never do that," said Bru. Then he hurried away to his house and slammed the door behind him.

"I say let's break down his door and see what's going on," said McWhiskers angrily.

"We can't do that to a friend," said Puddles. "Let's just knock on his door and ask to come in."

Bru's friends all went to his door. Puddles knocked. When Bru opened the door, there were all his friends.

"We want to know why you're deceiving us," said Tux. "You are, you know. What are you hiding?"

"Why would I do that to you guys?" said Bru. And with that, he slammed the door. Now what would you do if you had been one of his friends?

Usually, Puddles, doesn't get angry. He's quite a happy guy. But when Bru slammed the door in his face, Puddles became quite angry. He pounded on Bru's door until it seemed that it would fall down.

At last Bru opened the door. Puddles stuck his foot in the doorway.

"You don't do that to your good friends," said Puddles angrily.

Bru was so surprised that he couldn't slam the door

again. When his friends said, "May we come in?" he was still so surprised that he couldn't say no. So the friends all thought that meant yes.

"Wow! Look at that!" said McWhiskers.

On one side of the room were stacks and stacks of honey pots. There must have been dozens of them.

"So that's why you've been sneaking around," said Mc-Whiskers. "You've been taking honey from every honey tree in the forest. You have enough here for *ten* bears."

"And you're not leaving enough for others, especially the bees and the other bears," said KaWally.

"And you didn't want us to know, and so you have been deceiving us," said PJ. "Shame on you for being greedy, then

deceiving your friends about it."

Bru hung his head. "You're right," he said. "I've been greedy, and I have been deceiving my friends about it. I'm sorry. Will you help me?"

"Do what?" asked PJ.

"Take some of these honey

pots to the poor bear family across the valley," said Bru. "Some of this came from their trees."

Before long there was a parade of Bru and his friends, each carrying a big honey pot to the poor bear family. I sup-pose Bru was very careful after that not to deceive his friends again. I suppose you would be if you were Bru, wouldn't you?

Can You Crow
Like Me?

A Story About Pride

"Who are you?" Puddles asked. "Where did you come from?"

"Who am I?" the rooster said proudly. "Haven't you ever seen a rooster? Roosters are the most important birds of all. There is no bird in all the world that can crow like a rooster."

184

When he said that, the rooster gave a mighty crow. Puddles was sure that everyone in their little community could hear that. "Can you do that?" the rooster asked Puddles.

Puddles didn't think he could do that, but he thought he should try. I'm sure you have never heard a blue hippo trying to crow like a rooster. It really sounded quite silly.

The rooster laughed and laughed. "No, no, no!" he said. "Listen again." Then he let go with a terrific crow. It echoed all the way down the lane.

Before long Bru and McWhiskers came running down the path.

"What's that terrible noise?" Bru asked.

"It sounds like someone has a bad stomachache," said Mc-Whiskers.

The rooster was not happy to hear them say these things. "I am a rooster," he said. "I can crow a mighty crow. Can you do that?" Then the rooster crowed one of his best. Puddles thought it would shake the leaves from the trees.

Bru didn't think he could do that, but he certainly wasn't going to let this little rooster do something he couldn't do. So Bru tried. Even McWhiskers laughed to hear Bru crow like a rooster. It really wasn't a very good crow at all.

"All right, wise guy, you try it," Bru said to McWhiskers. But the best McWhiskers could do was a middle-size squeak. It wasn't at all like a rooster's crow.

"Do you see?" said the rooster. "Where I come from I wake up the community with crowing like this. Everyone thinks I'm very important. Not one of you can do it."

Bru looked ashamed. He didn't like it that a rooster could do something he couldn't do. McWhiskers and Puddles both looked ashamed, too. They didn't like having a rooster do something that they couldn't do.

"By the way, what *can* you do?" the rooster asked the three friends. "You, bear, what can you do?"

"Well, I...I...I gather honey and put it into honey pots," he said.

"What for?" said the rooster. "So you can eat it and get fat? What does that do to change the world?"

Bru looked even more ashamed now. What could he do? He certainly couldn't crow

like that rooster.

"And you, blue hippo, what do you do?" asked the rooster.

Puddles just looked at the ground, ashamed. He couldn't even think of a thing that he could do. He certainly couldn't crow like that rooster either.

"I know what you do, little mouse," said the rooster. "You squeak, eat cheese, and chew holes in things." Then the rooster laughed.

After the rooster laughed, he let go with a mighty crow. It almost shook the forest.

"We do much better things than crowing," McWhiskers said bravely. "In this little community, we help each other. You may not think that is important, but we do. Because we help each other, we get along well and don't make each other feel ashamed."

The rooster laughed and laughed. "Sounds important," he said. "But I don't need anyone to help me." With that, he let go with another terrific crow.

Bru and Puddles almost wished they could crow like that, but McWhiskers was angry. He headed home. So did Bru and Puddles.

For a long time the three friends could hear the rooster crowing down at the end of the path. Then suddenly the crowing stopped. Instead, they heard a squawking noise.

"Awwk! Help!" said the squawking noise.

The three friends ran to see what the squawking noise was all about. There was the rooster caught in a crude trap.

"Fox's trap," said Bru. "He's

got you."

"When he comes along, he will take you home to lunch," said Puddles. "But *you* will be the lunch."

"Give a big crow," said McWhiskers. "Maybe that will get you out of the trap. Or maybe it will help Fox know that you're caught in his trap. He will come running to eat you."

"No, no! Help me! Please!" begged the rooster. "That fox will eat me."

"But you said you don't need anyone to help you," said Bru.

"And you said it wasn't important for us to be helpers," said Puddles.

"And you made fun of us because we can't crow like you," said McWhiskers. "Perhaps we should make fun of

you now because you can't help yourself."

"Please, please help me," said the rooster. "You're right. It is much more important to help others than to crow."

"OK, little guy," said Puddles. "You made fun of me, but I'll help you." Puddles and Bru held the trap while McWhiskers opened the door.

"We'll all help you," said Bru.

"And I hope we've helped you learn not to be so proud," said McWhiskers. "You may crow better than we can, but we can open a trap to save your life."

Now the rooster looked ashamed. "Please forgive me," he said. "I did make fun of you. I was proud of my crowing. But you saved my life. Thank you. Thank you. Now I think I should go home where I belong."

Bru, Puddles, and McWhiskers watched the rooster walk down the path toward home. "I'm glad we can help each other," said Puddles. "That really is much more important than crowing."

It really is. You may not do something as well as a friend, but you can be a good helper. What is better than that?

A New Someone

A Story About Friendship

One morning Puddles met someone new as he was walking along the path near his home.

"Good morning, friend," said Puddles.

But the new someone said nothing.

Puddles was almost past the new someone when he realized that the new someone had said nothing. He hadn't answered Puddles at all.

Puddles stopped and went back to the new someone. "I said good morning and you didn't even answer me," said Puddles. "What kind of a new friend are you, anyway?"

But the new someone still said nothing.

"Well, if you won't answer when I say good morning, will you answer if I say hello?"

But the new someone said nothing.

"Is there something wrong with me?" Puddles demanded. "Don't you like me because I'm big? Or is it because I'm blue and you're yellow?"

But still the new someone said nothing.

"Oh, I know," said Puddles. "You're snooty. You don't like the kind of house I live in."

But the new someone said nothing.

"You're a little skinny, and you don't like me because I'm a little fat. That's it, isn't it?" Puddles asked.

But the new someone said nothing.

Puddles scratched his head. "OK, so it's not my house. It's not because I'm fat and you're skinny. It's not because I'm big and you're little. And it's not because I'm blue and you're yellow. But what is it? Why

don't you say hello to me?"

But the new someone said nothing.

"I know!" said Puddles. "I'm good at jumping rope and you're not! Or are you good at something that I'm not? What is it?"

But the new someone said nothing.

"Will you please say SOME-THING so I will know why you won't say ANYTHING?" Puddles shouted.

But the new someone said nothing.

"OK, if you won't talk, will you play ball with me?"

But the new someone said nothing.

"How about riding bikes with me?" asked Puddles.

But the new someone said nothing.

"How about a nice picnic

lunch?" asked Puddles.

But the new someone said nothing.

"I guess you just don't want to be my friend," said Puddles.

He felt so sad that some big tears began to roll down his cheeks.

Just then KaWally came by. "Why the tears, Puddles?" he asked his friend.

"I met this new someone, but he doesn't want to be my friend," said Puddles.

"How do you know?" asked KaWally. "Did he say so?"

"No," said Puddles. "He didn't do or say anything."

"Did he hit you or say something mean to you?" asked KaWally.

"No," said Puddles. "He didn't do or say anything."

"Did he tease you or take something away from you?" asked KaWally.

"No," said Puddles. "He didn't do or say anything."

"Hmmm," said KaWally. "Someone who doesn't want to be my friend will usually say so, or hit me, or say something mean, or tease me, or take something away from me," he said. "But I guess ignoring you is another way to say that he doesn't want to be your friend."

KaWally thought a minute. "Let me talk with this new someone. Let's see if he wants to be my friend."

When KaWally looked closely at the new someone, he began to laugh.

"What's so funny?" asked Puddles.

"Don't you see?" asked KaWally. "This is a scarecrow. He doesn't say anything because he can't say anything. Scarecrows can't talk."

"So he really may want to be my friend, but he can't tell me," said Puddles.

"That's right," said KaWally. "Why don't you shake his hand?"

Puddles shook hands with the scarecrow. "Each time I go by, I'll talk to you, even though you can't talk to me," he said. "We'll be good friends, even though you can't tell me what you want to say."

So Puddles and KaWally headed down the path. They turned to wave to the scarecrow, who probably wanted very much to wave back. But, of course, he couldn't.

It may be, it just may be, that some new someone really wants to be *your* friend but doesn't know how to say so. So it may be, it just may be, that you should do all you can to be that someone's friend anyway.

What do you think?

Lazy Syd Squirrel

A Story About Being Lazy

Bru and his friends had many interesting neighbors. In the forest where they lived there were several squirrel families. Each fall the squirrels worked very hard to store up acorns for the winter. When the snow fell on the forest, finding acorns was not easy.

That's why an older and wiser squirrel was surprised each day that fall to see Syd Squirrel playing. All the other squirrels were working from sunup to sundown gathering acorns and putting them away for the winter.

"Do you have all your

acorns in for the winter?" the older, wiser squirrel asked Syd one day.

"Haven't started yet," said Syd. "Lots of time! All my friends work, work, work. I figure a fellow needs a little time to play."

"All day every day?" the older, wiser squirrel asked.

"Need a little fun in life," said Syd. Then he closed his eyes and took a nap.

One morning big snowflakes began to fall in the forest. Syd looked outside. He looked at the calendar. The snow was early. He still had not started to gather acorns for winter.

Syd ran outside and began to gather acorns as fast as he could. But the snowflakes were falling faster now. Before long, the ground was white. Syd couldn't find the acorns without digging in the snow. When Syd got home that night, he was cold and sad. He had only a tiny bag of acorns instead of the big one he should have had.

"It's an early snow," said Syd. "Tomorrow will be a nice warm day."

But the next day was very cold. Syd went outside, but a sharp gust of north wind almost blew him over. He could stay outside only a few minutes.

Each day was either cold or snowy. Syd looked at his calendar. "Winter isn't supposed to be here yet!" he kept saying. But it was. Winter didn't go away either.

Syd looked at the few little sacks of acorns in the corner. What would he do? There were not enough to last all winter. He would get very hungry before spring. Syd began to worry that he might even starve.

One cold winter day Syd heard a knock at the door. When he opened it, he saw all the other squirrels in that part of the forest. Each one had a little sack of acorns.

"You were very fool-

ish," said the oldest and wisest squirrel. "You should have gathered your acorns instead of playing. I'm sure you realize that by now."

"I...I was *very* foolish," said Syd. "I do realize that now."

"Well," said the oldest and wisest squirrel, "we can't let you go hungry this winter. So we each have a little bag of acorns for you."

Tears came into Syd's eyes. What kind neighbors!

"Oh, thank you, thank you," Syd said again and again. "What wonderful neighbors you are."

So each squirrel in that part of the forest gave Syd a little bag of acorns. But lots of little bags are just as much as a few big bags. By the time the last squirrel had given Syd a little bag of acorns, Syd had all he needed for the winter.

Ever after that, Syd was the hardest working squirrel in the forest, gathering acorns for the winter. And each fall, he gathered an extra bag of acorns for any squirrel who was too old or too sick to gather as much as needed.

Accidents Do Happen

A Story About Bad Days

Some days are just not good days. In fact, some days are bad days. Puddles found that out one gloomy day when nothing seemed to go quite right.

"Good morning!" Puddles said when he saw Bru outside his door. But Puddles wasn't watching where he was going. He stepped on Bru's foot. I don't know what you would say if a blue hippo stepped on your foot early in the morning. I won't even tell you what Bru said. But it wasn't very nice.

Puddles was truly sorry about stepping on Bru's foot. But what could he do now except to say it?

"I'm really sorry, Bru," said Puddles. "Please forgive me."

"Why don't you watch where you're going?" Bru grumbled. "Why don't you get lost?"

Puddles was thinking about this when he walked down the path. He was thinking about it so much that he wasn't watching where he was going. So he

bumped into PJ and knocked
him flat on the ground.

"Oh, I'm terribly
sorry," said
Puddles.

"I was thinking about something. Please forgive me."

"Why don't you watch where you're going?" PJ yelled at Puddles. "Why don't you get lost?"

Now Puddles did feel sorry for himself. He sat on an old stump by the side of the road. He didn't even see KaWally come along.

So when KaWally said hi, Puddles was startled. He jumped up from the stump and accidentally knocked KaWally down.

"Oh, I'm terribly sorry," said Puddles. "Please forgive me!"

"Why don't you watch where you're going?" KaWally yelled. "Why don't you get lost?"

"It must be me," said Puddles. "I thought it was just a bad day. But there's something wrong with me. I'd better hide before I hurt someone."

Puddles ran into the woods to hide. But he didn't see Tux and Tux didn't see him, and so they crashed near a big tree. Tux fell flat on the ground.

"Oh, forgive me," said Puddles. "I didn't see you."

"Why don't you watch where you're going?" Tux yelled. "Why don't you get lost?"

Puddles was just getting up to run away and hide. He didn't see McWhiskers coming along. So when Puddles turned around to run, his arm caught McWhiskers and knocked him to the ground.

"Hey! Watch where you're going!" McWhiskers yelled.

"Sorry! I didn't see you!" said Puddles.

"Why don't you get lost?"

said McWhiskers.

Puddles was feeling so sorry for himself now that he ran and ran into the woods. Big tears ran down his blue cheeks. He didn't want to hurt his friends. He didn't want his friends to yell at him. At last Puddles saw a big log. He sat down on the log and closed his eyes. He pretended that none of these things had happened. He and his friends were playing ball in the

meadow and having fun. But no matter how much he pretended, Puddles knew that these things had happened. He was sure his friends would never want to be his friend again.

Suddenly Puddles felt something tapping on his knee. He was almost afraid to open his eyes. But he did.

There were Bru and PJ, KaWally and Tux, and even McWhiskers. Bru held a big red ball. "Hey! Time to play ball in the meadow," said Bru. "Don't sit out here feeling sorry for yourself. Let's go

have some fun."

"But...but I hurt all of you," said Puddles. "You all told me to get lost."

"So you got lost," said PJ. "Now we want you back."

"And we all forgive you," said KaWally.

"So get off that log and let's play ball," said McWhiskers.

It was really quite an exciting ball game. And Puddles didn't step on anyone's foot or knock anyone over.

We all have bad days, don't we? But we can turn bad days into good days. That's what Puddles would tell you.

Ten Times Better

A Story About Pride

You may have guessed by now that Bru likes to tease little McWhiskers. Sometimes Bru goes further than teasing. He often tries to make himself look bigger than he is by making McWhiskers seem smaller than he is.

The other day Bru was in one of these moods. "I can do anything ten times better than you," Bru bragged. "Can you lift that little rock over there?"

McWhiskers didn't really want to get started with this. But he picked up the rock to keep Bru happy.

Bru laughed. "Here's a rock ten times bigger," he bragged again. "Watch me lift it." Then Bru lifted it easily.

"How far can you jump?" Bru asked McWhiskers. "Let's see!"

McWhiskers really wanted to walk away. But he thought he should be polite to Bru. So he jumped as far as he could.

Of course, Bru jumped ten times higher and ten times farther than McWhiskers did. Then he laughed at McWhiskers.

"Here's a ball," said Bru. "Throw it."

McWhiskers threw the ball. Then Bru picked up the ball and threw it ten times farther than McWhiskers had thrown it.

"See!" said Bru. "Do anything! I'll do it ten times better than you. Come on, I challenge you."

Bru was becoming very proud now. He was bragging so much that McWhiskers wanted to run away and hide.

"Bru, I really don't want to do this," said McWhiskers. "You're ten times better than I am, and so let's leave it at that."

"CHICKEN!" shouted Bru.

"Chicken! Chicken! Chicken!"

McWhiskers wasn't going to argue with Bru. He quietly kept walking away.

Suddenly there was a strong gust of wind. Leaves blew across the path. Bru reached up to hold his hat on his head. But it was too late. The wind picked up Bru's hat and blew it up and up. Higher and higher went the hat. In a few moments it blew into the top of a big tree. The hat came to rest far out on a little limb.

"My hat! My hat!" cried Bru. "I can't live without my hat." Bru wrung his hands and cried

as if he had lost his best friend. "My hat! My hat!" he kept saying.

McWhiskers came back and watched Bru for a few minutes.

"Well, why don't you climb the tree and get your hat?" McWhiskers asked.

"Look where it is," said Bru. "I can climb to the top of the tree. But I could never climb out on that little limb." Then Bru kept wringing his hands and saying, "My hat! My hat!"

While Bru was doing this, McWhiskers quietly climbed up the tree and out on the little limb. At last he grabbed Bru's hat and sent it sailing down where Bru was standing.

"HERE COMES YOUR HAT!" McWhiskers shouted as the hat was sailing down.

"My hat! My hat!" Bru said happily. He picked up the hat

and started to walk away.

"HOLD IT!" McWhiskers shouted. "Don't move!"

Bru stopped. He looked up at McWhiskers, at the top of the tree and out near the end of the little limb.

"You bragged that you can do anything ten times better than I can do it," McWhiskers shouted. "Well, climb ten times higher than this and ten times farther out on a limb. I *dare* you! I *double dare* you!"

Bru looked down at the ground. "You're right!" he said. "I'm sorry."

Bru started to walk away. Then he stopped and waved to McWhiskers, who was down on the ground by this time. "Thanks for the hat!" he called.

"You're welcome," said Mc-Whiskers. "And thanks for saying thanks."

Who Can Build This Bridge?

A Story About Working Together

"Let's build a bridge across the stream here," said Bru. "That will save us an hour or more each time we go to the village."

Putting some big rocks at the right place was easy. But putting a big log across the stream was not easy. It wasn't even easy to pick up the log.

Everyone laughed when McWhiskers tried to lift the log. It was much bigger than McWhiskers. But he did lift it an inch or so from the ground.

Tux grunted and groaned, and he lifted the log two or three inches from the ground.

KaWally tried to lift the log.

He grunted and groaned, too. But he could lift one end of the log about six inches from the ground.

PJ did a little better. He lifted one end of the log about a foot from the ground. But that didn't get the log over to the stream.

Bru flexed his muscles. He picked up one end of the log. But he couldn't drag the log

across the ground.

Puddles picked up one end of the log and dragged it a few feet. But the stream was too far for him.

"If Bru or Puddles can't get the log over to the stream, who can?" PJ asked.

All the friends sat down on the log to think. KaWally thought they should hire an elephant to do it. But where would they find the elephant?

Everyone had an idea. But no one had a good idea.

So they all sat on the log some more, trying to think of a way to get the log over to the stream.

"There isn't one of us strong enough to put that log where it should go," said Puddles. "Not *one*."

"That's it!" said McWhiskers. "You just found a way."

Puddles looked puzzled. "I did?" he asked.

"Yes," said McWhiskers. "Not *one* of us can take the log where it should go. But all *six* of us can!"

Suddenly everyone realized what McWhiskers had said. So Puddles, Bru, PJ, KaWally, and Tux all rushed to one end of the log. Poor McWhiskers was left at the other end. You can guess what happened then.

"No, no, no!" said McWhiskers. "That won't work! Puddles, KaWally, and I will take one end. Bru, PJ, and Tux will take the other end."

You should have seen how easy it was to lift the log and carry it to the stream. Before long, the log was in place. The bridge was built.

There are many things that you can't do well alone. You need others to help you. When a job is too big for you alone, remember the log across the stream.

You Can't Catch My Ball

A Story About Bragging

"**Y**ou're really good at catching balls, Bru," said KaWally.

Bru and his friends liked to play ball in the meadow. It was fun to throw or kick the ball and see who could catch it. Bru was fast. He had big hands. So it was easy for him to catch the ball when it came his way.

"You could probably catch almost any ball," said Puddles.

"What do you mean *almost* any ball?" Bru asked. "I can catch *any* ball. There isn't a

221

ball on earth that I can't catch."

"I found a ball today that you can't catch," said Puddles.

"So did I," said KaWally. "That makes *two* balls that you can't catch."

"I can catch *any* ball on earth," Bru said again. "*Any* ball."

"No, you can't," said KaWally. "You can't catch the ball I found."

"And you can't catch the ball I found either," said Puddles.

"If I can't catch your balls, I'll give you each a big pot of honey," said Bru. "No, I'll give each of you *two* big pots of honey."

"You don't really want to do that, do you?" asked KaWally.

Bru laughed. "Of course, I don't," he said. "And I won't have to because I can catch

any ball on earth."

"I think you said that before," said Puddles.

"That sounds like you're bragging," said KaWally. "OK, since you want to brag so much, we'll take your pots of honey."

"Only if I can't catch your ball," said Bru. "Now, who is first?"

KaWally and Puddles led Bru down the path. Not far away KaWally stopped. He stooped down and picked something. Then he held it up. It was a big white dandelion ball.

"Do you see this ball?" asked KaWally. "You can't catch it." When he said that, KaWally blew on the white dandelion ball. Pieces of it flew into the air. The wind caught them, and before Bru could close his mouth, they were gone.

"It's not fair," said Bru. "You didn't even give me a chance. Do it again."

KaWally found another dandelion ball. "Ready?" he asked.

"Ready," said Bru. Then KaWally blew. Of course, the dandelion ball flew into a hundred pieces before Bru could even reach it. Bru stood there with his mouth open.

"Wait here," said Puddles. "I'll get my ball." Before long he came back from his house. He had a little jar in his hands.

"Watch," said Puddles. He reached into the jar and pulled out a little stick with a loop on it.

Puddles blew on the loop. A beautiful bubble came out. It looked like a ball with rainbows all over it.

"Catch it," said Puddles. He blew softly on the stick with the loop, and the beautiful rainbow ball drifted into the air. It drifted over Bru's head. Bru reached up. But the bubble was too high.

"That's not fair," said Bru. "Do it again."

So Puddles blew another bubble. It floated right in front of Bru's nose. Bru reached out to catch it. But the second he touched it the bubble burst. He could not catch the rainbow ball.

"I...I guess I need to give each of you two pots of honey," he said. "You had some balls I couldn't catch."

"Keep your honey," said Puddles. "I don't want it."

"Me neither," said KaWally. "All we want you to do is stop bragging."

"That's right," said Puddles.

"Bragging will get you in trouble. It almost cost you four pots of honey."

"I'm sorry," said Bru. "I was bragging. I will try not to do it again." And for a long, long time Bru really did try not to brag. But the next time he forgot is another story for another time. OK?

Six Doors

A Story About Doing Things Together

What a day for a hike! Puddles and his five friends were so happy that they could hike together in the forest. The sun was shining. The air was warm and breezy.

"And we're all together," said Puddles.

Puddles and his friends loved to do things together. They had all agreed that today would be their "together" day. Whatever they did all day, they would do it together.

"Nothing will keep us from doing things together today," said Puddles.

"Nothing!" the other five friends said.

There wasn't a cloud in the sky. It was bright and beautiful.

That is, there wasn't a cloud in the sky until nine o'clock. By ten o'clock the sky was filled with big white puffy clouds. By eleven o'clock the white puffy clouds had turned to dark rain clouds.

227

"We'd better get home," said Puddles. "Look at that sky. It's going to rain."

So the six friends headed home. By the time they reached the path the wind was blowing fiercely. By the time they reached McWhiskers's house the rain had started to fall in big drops.

"Come inside and we'll have our picnic lunch together," said McWhiskers.

But when the five other friends looked at McWhiskers's door, they shook their heads. "I'm much too big," said Tux. "I can't go in there."

"Neither can I," said KaWally.

And neither could any of the other friends. So McWhiskers would not go in either. Remember? They would stick together today, no matter what.

Next the six friends went to Tux's house. "Come inside and we'll have our picnic lunch together here," said Tux.

"I can come in with you," said McWhiskers.

"But the rest of us can't," said Puddles.

"Then I won't go in either," said Tux. "We're staying together. Remember?"

At KaWally's house, Tux and McWhiskers could go in with him. But PJ, Bru, and Puddles were too big.

"We will stick together," said Puddles.

So they all went to PJ's house. Of course, PJ could go inside. So could McWhiskers, Tux, and KaWally. But Bru and Puddles could not get through the door.

"We *will* stick together," said Puddles.

So they all went to Bru's house. Everyone could go through Bru's door except Puddles. He was too big.

"Remember? We *will* stick together today," said McWhiskers.

So they all went to Puddles's houseboat.

"Come aboard and come in," said Puddles.

McWhiskers went in.

Tux went in.

KaWally went in.

PJ went in.

Bru went in.

And then Puddles went in. Now all six friends were together. Now they could eat their picnic lunch together while it rained outside.

"I'm glad we stayed together," said Puddles. "It is much more fun to eat our picnic lunch together than all alone."

I'm sure you think that is more fun, too. Will you do something with others today?

231

Friends Are Friendly

A Story About Being Kind

"What is that thing coming down the path?" Bru asked.

Bru had never seen an elephant before. He certainly had never seen an elephant pulling a red wagon full of jars. Of course, the elephant had never seen a bruin bear before either. So when they met on the path, they stared at each other for a long time before they talked.

Suddenly Bru began to laugh. He laughed and laughed as he pointed at the elephant's ears.

"What are those things?" Bru said between laughs.

"Bru, that isn't very kind," said KaWally. "How would you like it if someone laughed at your ears?"

"If I had big silly ears like that, he should laugh at me,

too," said Bru.

The elephant frowned. He had never met anyone as rude and unkind as this, so he wasn't sure what he should do. The elephant decided he would do nothing.

But Bru wasn't through yet. "You're kinda plump, aren't you?" he said. Then he laughed and laughed again at the elephant. "You must be eating too many cookies or something. Or maybe you need to get some more exercise."

"Bru, really!" said KaWally. "How would you like it if someone laughed at you because of your size?"

"If I were a blimp like that, he should laugh at me," said Bru.

The elephant frowned. He was sure this must be the rudest person he had ever met.

He really didn't know what to do. So he didn't do anything.

Bru thought he was funny now. He didn't realize how rude he was to the poor elephant. So he kept on. "What size shoes do you wear, Tiny?" said Bru. Then he laughed at his own joke, which wasn't a very good joke either. "Or do you wear bushel baskets for shoes?"

KaWally didn't think it was very funny. The elephant didn't think it was very funny either. But Bru thought it was so funny that he laughed a long time.

"Bru, I'm ashamed of you," said KaWally. "Do you know how rude and unkind you are to this...this...whatever it is."

"I'm an elephant," said the elephant. "And what are you?"

"My name is KaWally," said KaWally. "I'm a koala bear."

"And what is that?" asked the elephant.

"Bru is a bruin bear," said KaWally. "He isn't always this rude. I'm sorry."

"Hey, don't talk about me like that," said Bru. "I'm just having some fun with this funny-looking thing. You have to admit, that thing is really weird. Look at his nose! Have you ever seen a nose like that?"

"Bru! Really!" said KaWally. "Shame on you."

"Well, what good is a long nose like that?" Bru asked. "What do you do with such a thing, anyway? And how many times do you step on your own nose?"

Bru thought that was funny, too. So he laughed some more.

"I'll show you what I can do with it," said the elephant. So he poked his trunk into a big tub of water sitting by the path.

Then he sprayed Bru until he was drenched.

"I came here from the other side of the forest to make friends," said the elephant. "I heard that some of you here like honey. All those pots are filled with honey. I brought it here as a love gift."

Bru's mouth fell open. "Well now, *friend*," he said. "I'm so glad to welcome you."

"Sorry, but friends are friendly," said the elephant. "You haven't been friendly. You have been unkind and rude. So I'm giving all that honey to your friendly friend KaWally."

Bru was still standing there with his mouth open as the elephant helped KaWally unload all the honey at his door.

Then the elephant waved good-bye to
KaWally and pulled his red wagon away.

"I...I guess I was a little rude," Bru
said to KaWally. "I...I guess I really
didn't deserve any honey. I guess
he's right, friends are friendly."

Do you think friends should
be friendly? Bru
thinks so
now!

Big, Ugly, Scary Footprints

A Story About Courage

KaWally, Tux, and PJ had nightmares after Bru told scary stories one night by the campfire. You probably would not have slept well either. You probably would have dreamed dreams with all kinds of monsters in them.

This scary monster stuff didn't seem to bother McWhiskers. He said cat stories scared him. But not all that monster stuff Bru talked about in his stories. Puddles didn't get scared because he didn't understand Bru's stories. He just didn't get what they meant. So how can you get scared of something if you don't understand what that something is? Anyway, Puddles was quite sure he must be as big as any monster in Bru's stories.

But to KaWally, Tux, and PJ these monsters seemed as big as a house. And they had feet

big enough to crush them.

KaWally put quilts over his windows before he went to bed. Tux pulled the covers over him and didn't come out until morning. And PJ slept under his bed.

The next morning KaWally decided he would go to Tux's house and see how he was. PJ had the same idea. So when Tux opened his door, there were his two friends.

"Am I glad to see you," he said. "I hardly slept all night."

"Me neither," said PJ.

"I had terrible nightmares," said KaWally.

"Let's go for a walk in the forest and forget Bru's scary stories," said Tux. That seemed like a good idea, so the three went for a walk in the forest.

The morning was gloomy and dark in the forest. The night fog had not lifted yet. Trees looked almost like giants standing here and there.

Tux began to shake. He was afraid of the gloomy forest. PJ was sure he saw a dark form among the trees. And KaWally said they should be on the lookout for monsters.

Suddenly as they came to an open area with soft dirt they stopped. "LOOK!" shouted PJ. "Do you see what I see?" There in the soft dirt were giant footprints. They had never seen footprints that large before. And they looked so strange, like no other footprints they had ever seen.

"I tell you there are *monsters* in this forest," KaWally whispered. "Bru was right," said KaWally. "His stories were about real monsters. They're here, in our own forest."

"LET'S GET OUT OF HERE!" shouted PJ.

The three friends started to run. But suddenly they stopped.

"LISTEN!" shouted KaWally.

"A MONSTER," shouted PJ.

"RUN! Run for your life," said Tux.

The three ran faster than they had ever run before. But they didn't run very far. Suddenly they stopped and were very quiet.

"Shhh!" said KaWally. "I

see it. It's in the fog over there." He pointed to a huge monstrous shape in the fog.

"IT'S COMING THIS WAY!" shouted PJ. "Quick, run the other way."

Once more the three started to run. Then a voice called out to them. "STOP!" said the voice.

The three wanted to run. But they couldn't. They were too scared. So they stopped. The monstrous shape came closer and closer.

"We're doomed!" Tux whimpered.

"It's going to get us!" whined PJ.

Then the voice called out again. "IS THAT YOU?" the voice said. "Will you please help me?"

At that very moment KaWally saw the shape of the monstrous thing. "Puddles!" he said. "Is that really you?"

"Yes, it is really me," Puddles answered. "Will you please help me get this thing off my foot?"

Puddles came crashing through the forest. He had a huge basket caught on one foot.

The three friends pulled together. They tugged and pulled. They grunted and groaned. At last they had the basket off. Then the four friends walked toward home.

"I...I feel a little silly now," said PJ. "I thought you were a monster, Puddles."

"I feel silly, too," said KaWally. "I was really afraid out there today."

"I think we were scared because we forgot to pray," said Tux. Then they all decided that Tux was right.

The next time you're afraid of something, remember Puddles's basket prints. Perhaps that will remind you to pray. Do you think so?

A Box for Fox

A Story About Honesty

"**L**ook at that!" said KaWally. "An apple on the path. Now where did that come from?"

"And there's another one up ahead," said Tux.

"And another farther ahead," said KaWally. "Quick, let's run home and get a box."

Before long, KaWally and Tux had a box. They began to pick up the apples.

"These are great apples," said KaWally. "I'm sure some-one must have dropped them.

Apples don't just grow on a path."

Every few feet, KaWally and Tux found another apple. Before long, the box was almost full of apples.

"Let's hide this box of apples behind that bush," said Tux. "Then we can run ahead to see if we can find the person who lost them."

So Tux and KaWally hid the box of apples behind a big bush. Then they ran ahead to

find the person who had lost them.

Before long, Tux and KaWally saw someone ahead on the path. But as they got closer, they stopped.

"Do you see who I see?" asked Tux.

"I see who you see," said KaWally. "It's *Fox*!"

"And do you see what Fox has over his shoulder?" asked Tux.

"I see what he has over his shoulder," said KaWally. "It's a bag. And apples are falling through a hole in his bag. The bag is almost empty."

"Well, now that we know it's Fox, we can keep the apples," said Tux. "He doesn't deserve them."

So Tux and KaWally ran back

to their box of apples. But while they were still behind the bush, they saw Fox running their way.

"My apples! My apples!" said Fox. "I've lost my apples. Where are they?"

Fox was looking on the path for his apples. But, of course, the apples were not on the path now. They were in the box that Tux and KaWally had hidden behind the bush.

Fox ran past the place where the two friends were hiding.

"Serves him right!" KaWally whispered.

"Yes, it does," said Tux. "And now we have a nice box of apples."

KaWally picked up an apple and began to munch on it. The first bite tasted good. But the second bite didn't seem to taste so good.

"What's the matter?" asked Tux. "Don't you like the apple?"

"The apple should taste wonderful," said KaWally. "But it doesn't. I...I guess I know the apples really belong to Fox."

Tux looked at KaWally. KaWally couldn't eat the apple.

"I...I think we're stealing these apples, Tux," said KaWally. "That's why they don't taste so good."

"I...I think you're right,"

said Tux. "We don't really want to eat someone else's apples, do we?"

Suddenly Tux and KaWally heard Fox coming back. He was still looking for his apples.

"My apples! My apples!" he kept saying. "I've lost my beautiful apples. My bag is empty. But where did they go?"

"THEY'RE HERE," KaWally shouted.

"We found them," Tux added.

Then Tux and KaWally brought the box out to Fox. "We were going to keep them," said KaWally. "But then we knew they were really yours. Here. Take them home."

Fox looked ashamed when he heard that. "If I had found your apples, I would have kept them," said Fox. "But you're giving my apples back to me. Thank you for being honest."

Fox gave Tux and KaWally each an apple to eat on the way home. Then he picked up the box of apples and went away.

"You know what?" KaWally asked Tux. "This apple really tastes wonderful."

"Mine, too," said Tux.

But then they should, shouldn't they?

Surprise Gifts

A Story About Giving

PJ was walking along the path when McWhiskers ran out to meet him. McWhiskers plopped a candle into his hand.

"SURPRISE!" McWhiskers shouted. Then he ran off toward PJ's house.

PJ wondered why McWhiskers gave him a candle. But he kept it and walked toward home. Suddenly Tux ran out to meet him. Tux plopped another candle into his hand.

"SURPRISE!" Tux shouted. Then he ran off toward PJ's house.

PJ wondered why Tux gave him a candle. But he kept it and walked toward home. Suddenly KaWally ran out to meet him. KaWally plopped a candle into his hand.

"SURPRISE!" KaWally shouted. Then he ran off toward PJ's house.

PJ's hands were getting full of candles. But he kept walking toward home. Suddenly Bru ran out to meet him. Bru plopped a candle into his hand.

"SURPRISE!" Bru shouted. Then he ran off toward PJ's house.

PJ hardly knew what to do with all the candles now. But he kept walking toward home. Suddenly Puddles ran out to meet him. Puddles plopped another candle into his hand.

PJ was ready to open his door to go into his house when he heard his friends nearby. "SURPRISE!" they shouted. Then all of PJ's friends stepped from behind a big bush where they had been hiding.

Bru was holding a big cake. He had a silly grin on his face.

"Happy Birthday to you!" PJ's friends began to sing.

PJ smiled a big smile. He had almost forgotten that this was his birthday because he thought his friends had almost forgotten that this was his birthday.

"SURPRISE!" Puddles shouted. Then he ran off toward PJ's house.

PJ was almost home now. His arms were filled with candles. He wondered why his friends had stuffed all these candles into his hands.

"Here!" said Bru. "Stick those candles on this cake and let's sing for you again."

Now PJ knew why they had given him all the candles. And PJ thought this must be about the best birthday ever. Perhaps that was because his friends had given him the most unusual birthday gifts ever.

By the way, if this is *your* birthday, HAPPY BIRTHDAY!

A Green Apple Tummyache

A Story About Being a Friend

"Did you hear about Puddles?" KaWally asked.

"What about Puddles?" McWhiskers replied.

"He has a giant tummyache," said KaWally.

"Because he has a giant tummy?" asked McWhiskers.

"No," said KaWally. "It's a much bigger tummyache than his tummy. That's why."

McWhiskers knew that it must really be quite a tummyache to be a bigger tummyache than Puddles's tummy. So he decided to go to Puddles's house to be a friend.

Puddles was in bed. He not only looked sick. He looked yucky sick. You've seen people look like that, haven't you?

"What's the problem?" McWhiskers asked. "Something you ate?"

"Green apples," said Puddles. "I have a green apple tummyache. I ate 18 green apples from that tree at the edge of the meadow."

"An 18-apple green apple tummyache," said McWhiskers. Then he whistled as well as an overgrown mouse can whistle. *"Wow.* No wonder KaWally called it a giant tummyache."

Just then Bru walked in. He was holding a brown paper bag. "I heard you have a tummyache," said Bru. "So I brought something for you. Works every time. My grandfather said it's the best thing you can take."

Puddles sat up in bed. "What...what is it, Bru?" he asked.

"Green apples," said Bru. Puddles is usually blue. But he almost turned green when he heard that. "OH, NO!" he shouted. "Please get those things out of here."

Of course, Bru didn't like that. "Well, of all the ungrateful people on earth," he growled. "I bring you a gift, and you don't even want to try it."

Bru didn't know that Puddles had an 18-apple green apple tummyache. If he had, he certainly would not have brought green apples to stop it. So Bru stormed out the door and went home.

Bru had just left when PJ walked in. "Looking a little green there, blue hippo," he said. "I hear you have a tummyache. I have a great cure. My uncle used it on all his children. It always worked."

PJ began to hammer on

Puddles's tummy with his hands, as if he were chopping it. "STOP! STOP!" shouted Puddles. "That feels terrible. It makes my tummyache worse."

PJ didn't like that. He stormed out the door angrily. "Well, some friend!" he mumbled. "I try to stop your tummyache, and you tell me to get out."

Just then Tux and KaWally

came in. "We have the best cure for your tummyache," they said. They held up a rope. "Let's go outside so you can jump rope," they said. "While we twirl it, you jump a hundred times. That will shake the aches out of you."

Puddles thought of jumping rope outside. But it made him more sick to think about it. "Get that rope out of here said Puddles. It makes my tummy hurt just to look at it."

"Well," KaWally grumbled. "Some friend."

"We try to help you, and you yell at us," said Tux.

When KaWally and Tux left, Puddles looked at McWhiskers. "I suppose you have a great cure for my 18-apple green apple tummyache, too," he said.

"I think I do," said Mc-Whiskers. "I think you should go to sleep and let your sleepy tummy take care of it. And I think you need a friend to sit here with you all night to keep you company."

Puddles smiled. "My tummy feels better already," he said. "You are a true friend. I think you have the best cure of all."

It was a long night for Mc-Whiskers. He really didn't get much sleep as Puddles tossed and turned. But at last both of them fell asleep.

Suddenly McWhiskers heard a voice shouting. "IT'S GONE! IT'S GONE!" the voice said. McWhiskers woke up and looked around the room. He was still in Puddles's house. "What's gone?" he asked. "Did someone steal something?"

"My 18-apple green apple tummyache is all gone!"

Puddles said. "It's gone, and you're still here. What a good friend you are to stay with me."

So, ever after, McWhiskers was known as the 18-apple green apple tummyache healer. It certainly takes a good friend to do that, doesn't it?

Gum

A Story About Greed

"Look what I found," said Puddles. "It's a big sack full of pretty packages."

"What's in the packages?" asked Tux.

"I don't know," said Puddles. "It says *bubble gum*. But what is bubble gum?"

KaWally pulled a little package of gum from the bag and smelled it. "It smells good," he said. "Something like honey."

"HONEY?" Bru shouted. "Let me smell one of those things."

Bru sniffed one of the packages of bubble gum. "It *does* smell something like honey," he said.

Without even asking Puddles, Bru began to tear the paper from packages of bubble gum. Then he popped each one into his mouth.

"Wait, wait, wait!" said KaWally. "You're being greedy. Why are you taking so many?

Don't you want to share with your friends?"

Bru didn't even answer KaWally. He kept tearing off paper and popping the bubble gum into his mouth.

Bru thought he would just chew this sweet stuff and swallow it. But by this time he had about a dozen or more hunks of bubble gum in his mouth. You just don't swallow a dozen

or more hunks of bubble gum in one gulp. You don't even swallow them in two or three gulps.

Suddenly Bru saw a big pink bubble come out of his

mouth. He had never seen a pink bubble gum bubble before. Bru had seen balloons before, so he thought it was like a big pink balloon. If you don't like a big pink balloon, you just reach up and punch it. That is, you would do that if you were a bruin bear. So that is what Bru did.

Bru didn't expect what came next. The pink bubble gum bubble stuck to his hand. Bru pulled his hand away, but a long string of gum came out after his hand.

Bru wasn't sure what to do next. So he reached up with his left hand and tried to pull the gum away from his right hand. But you know what happened next, don't you? The pink gum stuck to his left hand. When he pulled it away, he had a long string of pink

gum from his mouth to his right hand. He also had a long string of pink gum from his right hand to his left hand.

Now what? Bru didn't have any more hands, so he did what anyone would do. He sat down on the ground and tried to get the gum away with his right foot.

You do know what happened next, don't you? Bru had a long string of gum from his mouth to his right hand. He had another from his right hand to his left hand. Now he had another from his left hand to his right foot.

You might think that Bru would stop there and try to solve this mess. But he didn't. Without thinking, he put his left foot over to his right foot to try to get the gum away from it.

By this time everyone in the community was there, watching this wonderful sight. "Do you think he will get his left foot full of gum, too?" KaWally whispered.

"Yep, looks like that's what he's trying to do," said Tux.

"Shhh, this is getting interesting," said PJ. "I don't want to miss the show."

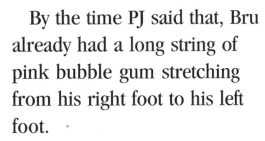

By the time PJ said that, Bru already had a long string of pink bubble gum stretching from his right foot to his left foot.

"It's really quite creative," said Puddles. "Kinda pretty."

"Come on, fellas," said McWhiskers. "We must rescue our greedy friend."

Bru quietly watched as McWhiskers took a big stick and began to wind the gum onto the stick. It took a long time, but Bru was free at last.

"Thank you, little friend," said Bru. "I really was greedy, wasn't I? I'm sorry."

Do you think Bru will be more careful the next time he wants to be greedy?

King for a Day

A Story About Serving

"Let's have a king for a day," said KaWally.

"What does a king for a day do?" asked Bru.

"He's the boss," said KaWally. "He's the one in charge of our little community for that day."

"I guess you would want me, of course," said Bru. "I mean, is there really anyone else?"

"You can't just make your-self king," KaWally said angrily. "What kind of king is that? We have to elect a king. We have to vote for our king."

Bru frowned. He wasn't sure his friends would vote for him. But what could he say? "Oh, all right," said Bru. "Let's hurry up and vote me in as king."

"NOT SO FAST," KaWally shouted. He was even more angry with Bru now. "We'll each give a campaign speech. We must each tell why we want to be king for a day."

Bru grumbled and growled. He thought his friends should just put a crown on him. Why all the speeches?

But Bru decided to go along with the speeches. What harm could there be?

"We'll start with the biggest and go down to the smallest," said KaWally. "You're first, Puddles." KaWally set up a big crate like a speaker's podium. He put a little crate behind it for each speaker to stand on.

"I...I...uh...I guess

you should make me king because I'm the biggest," said Puddles. Then he smiled a silly smile and sat down.

Bru was next. "I want to be king so I can make you guys bow down before me," he said. "If you don't know that I'm the smartest, most hand-some, most kinglike of all of you, you must be crazy." Then

Bru growled a nasty growl and sat down.

PJ thought he should be king because he had stripes. He thought every good king should have stripes, especially black-and-white stripes.

KaWally said he should be king because it was his idea. Tux said he should be king because he was the best dressed. Since he already looked like someone in a tuxedo, he wouldn't have to change into kingly things.

"What about you, McWhiskers?" KaWally asked. "You need to give your speech."

McWhiskers stood on the box. But he was so short that he was hidden behind the speaker's box.

"If I were king, I guess I would just want to help my friends have a great day," he said. "I guess I would just want to help you have a lot of fun and do good things today."

Puddles looked at Bru. Bru looked at PJ. PJ looked at KaWally. KaWally looked at Tux. Tux looked at McWhiskers. Then everyone looked at McWhiskers.

"HE'S OUR KING!" they all shouted together. "McWhiskers is our king for the day."

So McWhiskers called together his subjects to see what fun things they could all do together that day.

Do you think McWhiskers made the best king? Why?

A Night in the Woods

A Story About Truthfulness

"**W**here are you going?" KaWally asked.

"Camping in the forest tonight," said Puddles.

"Aren't you afraid?" asked KaWally. "You wouldn't get me

to go out in that forest at night. No way!"

"I'm not afraid of anything," said Puddles. "Look how big I am. Nothing is ever going to bother me."

Puddles walked toward the forest with his tent rolled up under one arm. Under his other arm he held his blanket. And he carried a lighted lantern. It wasn't like a flashlight. Puddles had to light this lantern with a match.

"Have fun!" KaWally called after him. "See you in the morning...I hope."

"Don't try to scare me," said Puddles. "I'm not afraid of anything in there."

Far out in the dark forest, Puddles set up his tent. He spread his blanket inside the tent. Then he set his lantern in one corner. He had lighted the lantern back home and carried it here that way. Don't ask me why. But that's the way he did it.

By the time all of this was done, it was almost dark. Puddles sat on an old log near the tent and watched as it grew darker and darker. At last he couldn't even see the trees. All he could see was the yellow glow of the light from his tent.

Suddenly Puddles heard a sound in the forest. It sounded like someone, or something, walking.

"Who...who's there?" he asked. But no one answered. The sound went the other way until Puddles couldn't hear it.

Puddles was afraid. What if this thing...whatever it was...came back? What if it was big and hairy? What if it was green and slimy and liked to eat blue hippos? Puddles began to think all kinds of scary thoughts.

Then Puddles heard a strange noise, like the noise of big wings swishing. They stopped just above his tent.

"Who...who's there?" he asked. But no one answered. The sound swished again the other way until Puddles couldn't hear it.

If that big green slimy hippo eater doesn't get me, the flying monster will, Puddles thought. All kinds of

fearful thoughts began to go through his mind again.

Puddles decided he should go into his tent. But he knew that big green slimy hippo eaters might even eat his tent. Or that flying monster might fly away with his tent. Then he would be left alone in the woods with nothing but his lantern.

As Puddles was worrying about these things, he heard a moaning in the pine trees nearby. "Is that the wind, or is someone moaning?" he croaked. He was really afraid now. Then he saw a bright flash of light. A moment later he heard a deep rumbling noise.

"Lightning! Thunder!" he whispered. "I would come out here on a night with a storm." Puddles knew he couldn't head home now. He might get caught in the storm. It would be better to stay in his tent.

Puddles tried to lie on his blanket and cover up with it as well. But there was hardly enough blanket to lie on.

Suddenly he saw another flash of light and heard another rumble of thunder. They were closer this time. Then there were another and another. Each time they were closer. Then big drops of rain began to fall on the tent. The wind pulled at the tent as if it were trying to blow it down.

Before long, the rain came down in torrents. The wind blew until Puddles thought his tent would blow over. Then a gust of wind blew through the tent. With one POOF his lantern blew out.

Puddles knew now that he should have brought along the

matches to light his lantern. He had no way to light it again until he went home. He would have to camp here in darkness while the storm raged outside.

Puddles lay on his blanket in the dark while the lightning flashed and the thunder rumbled and the rain beat down on his tent. Then he pulled the blanket over him.

At last the storm began to wear itself out. Tired and shaking, Puddles fell fast asleep.

That night, as you might guess, Puddles had many bad dreams. He dreamed of monsters attacking him. He dreamed that he was drowning in a torrent of water. And he dreamed of creatures in the big pine trees.

Then Puddles dreamed he heard footsteps. He dreamed that someone pulled aside his tent flap. He even dreamed that someone called his name. That someone kept calling his name.

Suddenly Puddles woke up. There was KaWally, standing with the tent flap pulled aside.

"Quite a night," said KaWally. "You must have really been scared."

Puddles didn't want to admit that he had been afraid. So he lied. "Who, me?" he said. "Why should I be afraid? Of course, I wasn't afraid. What was there to be afraid of?"

"Weren't you a tiny bit afraid?" KaWally asked. "Just a tiny bit?"

Puddles started to lie again. But he couldn't do it. "I was terribly afraid!" he said. Then he told KaWally all that had happened to him.

Puddles felt much better as

he and KaWally walked back through the wet woods toward home. He couldn't lie to his good friend. He knew he would feel terrible for a long time. Anyway, it really was fun telling his friend KaWally about all the spooky adventures in the forest that night. I think if you ever visit Puddles, he will tell you about these things. He will even tell you that he was afraid, not just a tiny bit, but lots and lots. And he may even ask you to come with him to camp out in the dark forest some night. Would you like to do that?

Sweet Songs

A Story About Praising God

You might be surprised to know that KaWally plays the guitar. Actually, he is quite good. Most of the time he likes to slip off quietly and play alone. KaWally would not be happy on the stage. He would not like to play in a big auditorium for thousands of people. He just likes to play.

One day KaWally opened his window and looked at the beautiful sunrise. "What a day!" he said. "I feel like singing praises to God for making such a beautiful day!" Have you ever gotten up in the morning and felt like that? I'm sure you have.

KaWally fixed a wonderful breakfast. It smelled so good. It's the kind of breakfast that makes you feel like jumping out of bed or running out to play with friends.

"What a day!" he said again. "I feel like singing praises to God for making such a beautiful sunny day!"

After breakfast KaWally hurried outside to enjoy the beautiful day. When he did, he heard the birds singing. The breezes were blowing softly in the trees. And the warm sunlight was beginning to feel like a soft blanket. KaWally even smelled the sweet smell of flowers nearby.

"What a day!" he said. "I feel

like singing praises to God for making such a beautiful day!"

That did it! That was the third time he said this. KaWally went inside for his guitar. He took his guitar to a little clearing out in the forest. There, all alone, he began to play his guitar and sing to God.

Thank You, God,
I want to say.
Thank You, God,
For this bright day.
Thank You, God,
With song I sing.
Thank You, God,
For everything.

KaWally sang one praise song after another. It was a day for soft notes of praises. He did not sing too loud. He did not sing too fast. But he did sing well.

Suddenly KaWally heard another voice singing with him. He looked up. A beautiful bird had heard his song and wanted to join him.

Then he heard another voice and another and another. Dozens of beautiful birds joined him from dozens of branches of dozens of trees. Then even more voices began to join in the songs. KaWally looked around. Animals of the forest had gathered to join him in his songs of praise to the Creator.

There were chipmunks, deer, raccoons, beavers, and almost every animal you would expect in the forest. One by one they joined with their own voices in the songs KaWally sang.

You might expect that KaWally would stop. Would he want to sing with all these forest folk?

But it was all too beautiful. KaWally could not stop. Instead,

the voices of all the forest animals singing together like a beautiful choir made KaWally want to sing even more praises to the God who made them all.

It seemed to KaWally that the sighing wind in the trees joined softly in the choir. The leaves seemed to rustle at the right time. The grasses and bushes growing in the forest seemed to bow when they should. I know you would have sat quietly to listen to this beautiful choir. Of course, the forest creatures would not have sung if any of us people had been there, would they?

One by one the forest choir members finished their songs and slipped back into the forest. The great choir, little by little, muffled softly into a solo.

KaWally was there all alone. He sang one last song of praise as the sighing wind seemed to say Amen. Then KaWally walked softly through the forest toward home. He could not say one word.

Just before KaWally reached home he met Bru.

"HI YA, PAL!" Bru shouted.

KaWally

smiled at Bru. "Shhh," he said softly, putting his finger to his lips. Then he slipped quietly inside his house, leaving Bru out on the path wondering what that was all about.

A Moonlight Picnic

A Story About Having Fun, Even When Things Aren't Fun

"Now don't forget, our picnic is at noon!" said McWhiskers. "Puddles, are you remembering all this?"

"I'm remembering," said Puddles. "Just be sure you're ready." It was Puddles's turn this morning to go into the village to get the food for the picnic. What would a picnic be without food?

McWhiskers asked Puddles to remember because sometimes Puddles let things distract him. Bru said he wasn't very responsible. When he was supposed to do *this,* he might get interested in *that* and forget to do *this.* You would never do that, would you?

"Let's all be at the meadow at noon," said McWhiskers. "Can you be back by then with the food, Puddles?"

"I can do it," said Puddles. "Just be sure you're there."

At noon, McWhiskers was spreading a big blanket out in the grassy meadow. Bru was already there. He was always early for picnics.

KaWally was coming across the meadow. PJ was coming down the path. And Tux was just coming out of his house. But Puddles wasn't anywhere to be seen.

By one o'clock, McWhiskers and his friends had spread out blankets and things for the picnic. And they had played three games. But Puddles was still not there.

By two o'clock, they had taken a hike and played three more games. But Puddles was still not there.

By four o'clock, Bru's stomach was growling. When Bru's stomach growled, Bru growled. "Wait till I get my hands on that overgrown stuffed shirt," said Bru. "I'll teach him not to keep us waiting."

By six o'clock, PJ and Bru were ready to go home and forget the picnic. But they kept thinking of the food. They were sure if they went home, Puddles would come with the food. But he didn't.

Bru and McWhiskers and their friends did not know that Puddles had found a carnival in the village. When he saw that, he forgot about the picnic. He went on the merry-go-round. He went on the Ferris wheel.

He went on a dozen other rides. He did not think once about the picnic until he was eating an ice cream cone.

"Oh, no!" he moaned. "I did it again. I got into other things. I forgot to get the picnic food. My friends have been waiting all afternoon for me. I'm in *big* trouble."

By this time, it was six o'clock. Puddles ran to the store and got the picnic food. Then he raced back to the forest as fast as he could go. But it took a long time to get back. By the time he reached the meadow, it was starting to get dark.

Puddles knew that his friends would be angry with

him. And they were. "I'm so sorry," he said. "I did it again. I let other things keep me from doing what I should."

PJ shouted at Puddles.

KaWally yelled at him.

Tux said a few unkind words about friends who forget their friends and do other things.

And Bru was just plain nasty.

But McWhiskers felt sorry for Puddles. He knew the problem Puddles had.

Everyone spread the food out on the blankets. But it was getting quite dark by this time.

"What fun is this?" Bru growled.

"Let's just choke our food down and go home," said PJ. "Puddles has spoiled this picnic."

They yelled at Puddles again. Or they thought they did. Puddles wasn't there.

Then they saw him sitting alone on a big log at the edge of the meadow. His head was in his hands. They could hear him sobbing. "Puddles may have spoiled our afternoon," Mc-Whiskers said angrily. "But you guys are spoiling our picnic. Will you stop grumbling and start having some fun?"

Everyone was quiet for a long time. Then suddenly KaWally shouted, "LOOK!"

The moon was coming up. It was a big full moon. Soon the whole meadow was bathed in silver moonlight.

Bru went over to the big log and sat down with Puddles. "Come on, Puddles. Let's make this the most fun picnic we've ever had," he said. "We can do it."

"Bru is right," said PJ.
"We've never had a moonlight
picnic before. Let's make it the
best ever."

Soon everyone was playing
games and eating food and
doing what friends do at picnics. You would have thought
it special to do all these things

in a big meadow in the light of
a big, glowing, full moon.

Much later, the friends
packed up their things and
headed home. "You know
what?" Bru said. "This really
was the best picnic ever.
Maybe our next picnic should
be a moonlight picnic, too."

Do you think it was?

A Pail of Purple Paint

A Story About Controlling Yourself

"You absolutely *must* see what I have," PJ said to KaWally. "It is the most beautiful stuff in the world."

"In that can?" asked KaWally. "It doesn't look very beautiful from here."

"The can isn't beautiful," said PJ. "It's what's in the can."

PJ put the can on the ground. Then he opened the lid. "Look at that!" he said. "Have you ever seen anything so beautiful?"

"What is it?" asked KaWally.

"Purple paint!" said PJ. "I have a special paintbrush to paint things purple. Watch this." PJ dipped the paintbrush into the purple paint. Then he swished the purple paint on his door.

"Isn't that just the most beautiful stuff you ever saw?" PJ asked.

KaWally looked at the purple door. "I think you said that before," he answered.

"Get some of our friends," said PJ. "I know they will be

more impressed than you are."

KaWally ran to find McWhiskers. By the time he brought McWhiskers back to see the purple paint, PJ had painted the rest of his house purple.

"Isn't that the most beautiful stuff you ever saw?" PJ asked.

"Be careful, McWhiskers," said KaWally. "He will paint you purple next."

"Get some more of our friends," said PJ. "I know they will be more im-

pressed than you two are."

KaWally and McWhiskers ran to find Tux. By the time they brought him back to see all the purple paint, PJ had painted the big tree next to his house. I suppose you have never seen a purple tree. Tux had never seen a big purple tree either.

"Isn't that the most beautiful stuff you ever saw?" PJ asked.

Tux looked at the purple tree. "Yuck!" he said. "That looks terrible!" KaWally and McWhiskers were too surprised to say anything.

"Get some more of our friends," said PJ. "I know they will be more impressed than you three are." Tux, KaWally, and McWhiskers ran to find Bru. By the time they brought him back to see the purple paint, PJ had painted the path

in front of his house.

"Isn't that the most beautiful stuff you ever saw?" PJ asked.

"You'd better get that ugly stuff away from him before he ruins the whole neighborhood," Bru growled.

"Get some more of our friends," said PJ. "I know they will be more impressed than you four are."

"There's only one left," said Bru. "He's blue. Maybe he will be more impressed with that gook than we are."

So Bru, Tux, KaWally, and McWhiskers ran to find Puddles. By the time they brought him back to see the purple paint, PJ had painted the bushes across the path.

"What's all that ugly stuff?" asked Puddles. PJ didn't like to hear that.

"It's the most beautiful stuff

you ever saw," he said.

"I still think we'd better get that stuff away from him before he ruins the neighborhood," Bru growled.

But it was too late. All the purple paint was gone. PJ had painted until he had used it up.

"Maybe you're too close to it," said Bru. "Come with us."

Bru and his friends led PJ down the path. "Now turn around and let's go back toward your house."

On the way back, PJ saw the blue sky up above. He saw the green trees along the road. He saw the green bushes, too. And he saw his friends' houses with their soft, pretty colors. Then suddenly PJ saw the purple mess up ahead.

"What do you think of it now?" asked Bru.

"I think it looks terrible," said PJ. "I didn't realize I was putting so much purple on everything. I didn't control myself very well."

"Well, let's get the garden hose and see if we can clean it off," said Bru. Bru didn't know that it was a water-based paint. He didn't know much about paint. He was just hoping that this would work.

PJ hurried to get the garden hose. "Oh, I hope this works," he said. "It looks more terrible the more I look at it."

PJ and Bru sprayed the house, the tree, the path, and the bushes. Before long, the purple paint was running off everything. PJ was so happy when he saw the green tree and green bushes again. He was so happy when he saw the path and his house the way they had been.

"I guess purple can be pretty if there isn't too much purple," said PJ.

"Sometimes a little is better than a lot," said McWhiskers. "I think you learned something today about controlling yourself." Do you think PJ learned that? Did you?

The Great Race

A Story About Pride

"Come on, slowpoke," Mc-Whiskers called to Bru. Bru, McWhiskers, and their friends had enjoyed their hike, but Bru was getting a little slow on the way back. He said he was just enjoying the scenery. Mc-Whiskers thought he was getting tired.

"Slowpoke, huh?" Bru growled. "I can run faster than you any day. I can run faster than you if I have my left foot tied to my right hand. I can run faster than you if I have my left foot tied to my right hand and I'm running backward."

Bru had a problem. He often said something like that without thinking about it. He was just beginning to see how that would work when McWhiskers spoke up.

"OK, I accept!" said McWhis-kers. "You all heard what Bru said, didn't you? Now he must do it."

Bru felt a little silly. He knew

299

that his pride was hurt when McWhiskers called him slowpoke. He wished that he hadn't said that. But he had. He couldn't get out of it without hurting his pride.

"All right, I'll do it!" Bru said. He was still letting his pride get in the way.

When the friends reached home, they got some rope. They tied Bru's left foot *up* to his right hand. Bru thought they should tie his right hand *down* to his left foot. But they all said that wasn't what he promised to do.

PJ was the referee because they all thought his stripes made him look like a referee. "OK, the race will be to that tree," he said, pointing to a tree down the path. "Whoever gets to that tree first wins."

Bru growled a little when he thought of the race. He wanted to say, "I quit." But his pride would not let him do it.

"On your mark, get set...GO!" said PJ.

Bru went three hoppity steps backward before he fell flat on his back. By that time McWhiskers was halfway to the tree. Then Bru tried again. But he got his right foot tangled in the rope that tied his left foot *up* to his right hand. What a mess! Bru was a pile of rope and bear lying on the path.

By that time McWhiskers reached the tree. The great race was over.

Now Bru was ashamed that he had said such a silly thing. He was even more ashamed that he had tried to do it. Why hadn't he admitted how foolish it was? Why did he make himself look so silly?

Bru's friends laughed and laughed as they untied him. They laughed as they teased Bru about his great race.

"Next time we'll tie both feet and hands together," said KaWally.

"Maybe we should just tie his mouth shut," said Tux. "Then he wouldn't say such silly things."

The friends laughed all the way home. Bru sat down on a big log by the side of the path to think about his pride.

"I guess I must have more mouth than brains," Bru grumbled to himself. "Why does my pride make me do things like that? I'm just a silly old bruin bear, that's all. All my friends are laughing at me."

"Not *all* of them," a voice said. Bru turned around. McWhiskers had quietly come behind him.

"I'm sorry, Bru," said McWhiskers. "You did let your mouth get you in trouble. And you do need to work on your pride. But I'm still your friend, and I won't laugh at you."

Bru looked at his little friend. McWhiskers had climbed up on the log and was sitting beside him.

"I'm glad you're my friend," said Bru. "Every time I see you I'll remember the great race. And I'll remember to be careful about my pride." That's really a good idea, isn't it?

Who Stole Bru's Gold Watch?

A Story About Forgiveness

"ALL RIGHT, EVERYONE! GET OUT HERE ON THE DOUBLE!" Bru shouted so loudly that it seemed he would shake all the trees of the forest.

It was barely sunrise. Some of Bru's friends were just getting up. But that didn't matter to Bru. He was demanding that his friends get outside where he could talk with them.

Before long, all of Bru's friends were sitting on the big logs in the clearing. Bru stood in the middle. He was angry.

"Last night there was a crime here," he growled. "Last night while I slept, someone broke into my house. The little crook stole my gold watch."

Bru's eyes were flashing. His teeth were bared. He looked nasty. "And I know which *one of you* did it!" he snarled.

"Which one of *us*?" KaWally asked. "You don't think one of your friends would steal your gold watch, do you?"

"I don't *think* one of my so-called friends would steal my gold watch," said Bru. "I

304

know which one of you stole it."

When he said that, Bru rushed over to McWhiskers. He pointed his finger at Mc-Whiskers, pushing it against his nose.

"*Here* is our thief," Bru growled. "*You* stole my gold watch, you little thief!"

McWhiskers was so shocked that he couldn't answer. The other friends were so shocked that they couldn't talk either. "I...I...I..." McWhiskers started to say. But he couldn't say anything more.

"Just a minute, Bru!" KaWally snapped. "Why do you think McWhiskers stole your watch?"

"OK, come with me," Bru answered. Then he led the others to his house. There was a hole dug under the side of the house.

"Just the right size for this thieving little rat," Bru growled. "You can't get in there, Puddles, can you? You can't either, PJ or KaWally or Tux, can you? That little thief is the only one who could go through that hole."

Then Bru stuck his big nose up to McWhiskers's little nose. "Now get out of this community," he growled. "We don't want little watch thieves living here with us."

The others felt sad as they saw McWhiskers start slowly down the path. They felt even

more sad when they saw big tears coming down his cheeks.

"SHAME ON YOU, you mean old bear," KaWally shouted at Bru. "You make a good bully. But you don't make a good detective, do you?"

"What do you mean?" Bru asked.

"I mean you said some terrible things to McWhiskers about stealing your watch," said KaWally. "But you didn't bother to look at the footprints all around this hole."

Bru looked down at the soft dirt that had been dug from the hole. There were dozens of footprints.

"Are those McWhiskers's footprints?" KaWally asked angrily.

Bru looked ashamed now. "*Fox*!" he said. "Fox made that hole. He stole my watch. After him."

They ran as fast as they could go toward Fox's house.

But before they reached it, they saw Fox ahead. Fox saw them, too. He dropped Bru's gold watch and ran home as fast as he could go.

"My watch!" said Bru. "I have my watch back." Then suddenly Bru remembered. "McWhiskers! Oh, no!" said Bru. "I must find him."

You should have seen Bru run as fast as he could go. He didn't have to run far, though.

He found McWhiskers sitting alone on a big log. Bru sat down and put his arm around McWhiskers.

"I don't deserve to be your friend," said Bru. "Fox took my watch. I got it back. Will you please forgive me for all the mean things I said?"

McWhiskers looked up and smiled. "I forgive you!" he said. "Now why don't we all have a fun picnic together today."

So that's what they did. Oh, by the way, Fox was not invited.

Joyful Noise™

A Story About Praise

McWhiskers opened his window. He looked out at the bright sunshine. He saw the spring flowers blooming on the hillside near his house. The sky was blue. The grass was green. Everywhere he looked he saw a special sight.

"I must do something today to praise God for *sight*!" he said. "But what can I do that is special?"

Tux opened his window. He smelled the apple blossoms on the tree near his window. He smelled the freshness of the air. And he smelled some bread baking in PJ's house. Tux sniffed again and again. It seemed that there were won-

derful smells everywhere.

"I must do something today to praise God for *smells*!" he said. "But what can I do that is special?"

KaWally opened his window. He heard the birds singing. He heard the wind sighing in the leaves of the big tree near his window. He heard wonderful sounds of spring everywhere.

"I must do something

today to praise God for *sounds*!" he said. "But what can I do that is special?"

PJ opened his window. The sights and smells and sounds came toward him. Then he picked up some of the fresh bread he had baked and began to eat it. It was so good. He thought of all the wonderful things he would taste that day.

"I must do

something today to praise God for *taste*!" he said. "But what can I do that is special?"

Puddles opened his window. The sights and smells and sounds came toward him, too. He tasted some of his wonderful breakfast. He was so happy for this beautiful spring day that he began to touch everything he could. How wonderful everything felt! "I must do something today to praise God for *touch*!" he said. "But what can I do that is special?"

Bru opened his window. The sights and smells and sounds came toward him, too. He tasted some of his wonderful breakfast. He was so happy for this beautiful spring day that he began to touch everything he could. How wonderful everything looked and smelled and sounded and tasted and felt!

"I must do something today to praise God for *sight* and *smells* and *sounds* and *taste*, and *touch*!" he said. "But what can I do that is special?"

Then Bru had an idea. He remembered the horn he had played at the beginning of this book. He remembered the uniform he had worn for that scene. He ran to his closet and put on his uniform. Then he rushed from his house, marching and playing.

"Praise the Lord!" he said between toots on his horn.

Before long, Puddles was there with his horn and his uniform. He hopped and played. Then he stopped long enough to shout, "PRAISE THE LORD!"

Wearing his uniform, PJ came out with his cymbals. KaWally appeared with his horn, too. They skipped and played joyfully.

Tux ran toward the front of the line with his sign that said JOYFUL NOISE. And McWhiskers ran in front of Tux with his baton, twirling it to lead the little band.

"PRAISE THE LORD!" they all shouted. "Praise Him for *sight* and *smells* and *sounds* and *taste* and *touch*. Praise Him for making our wonderful world."

Maybe you would like to join this happy little band and say, "Praise the Lord for everything." If you would, it's OK, even if it isn't the beautiful day that it was in the land of Joyful Noise.

With horns to toot
  And songs to sing,
With things that clang
  And some that ring,
We prance and dance
  On tippy toes,

And make a happy sound
That grows.
We sing a song
For girls and boys,
So you may call us
Joyful Noise.™

INDEX OF LESSONS

Pride

Self-Control

Self-Image

Serving Others

Sharing

Stubbornness

Thankfulness

Truthfulness

Worry